DECENT PEOPLE

By Donella Dunlop

FICTION

Menominee, The Wild River People
Sagganosh, The Britisher
Mittigoush, The French

NON-FICTION

Ed Dunlop, a Memoir
A Soldier's Story

DECENT PEOPLE

A Novel

DONELLA DUNLOP

Order this book online at www.trafford.com
or email orders@trafford.com

Most Trafford titles are also available at major online book retailers.

Printed in the United States of America.

ISBN: 978-1-4269-4660-8 (sc)
ISBN: 978-1-4269-4661-5 (e)

*Our mission is to efficiently provide the world's finest, most comprehensive book publishing
service, enabling every author to experience success. To find out how to publish your book,
your way, and have it available worldwide, visit us online at www.trafford.com*

Trafford rev. 10/26/2010

 www.trafford.com

North America & international
toll-free: 1 888 232 4444 (USA & Canada)
phone: 250 383 6864 ♦ fax: 812 355 4082

For my sister, Catherine Dunlop

CONTENTS

ACKNOWLEDGEMENTS

Special thanks to the Convent of Mary Immaculate, Pembroke, Ontario former school friends who shared with me their memories of golden days. Thanks also to my sisters, Janet Brennan and Maureen Havey, who helped me recall precious childhood memories.

You inspired the story but no one character in it is based on any one real person.

BOOK I

Chapter 1

RASPBERRIES

1958

Summer Wind swishes its way through bending meadow grasses. The birch trees bordering the meadow sway and whisper. The air is hot and dry against Anna's skin. Her eyes feel gritty. She squints. This is not her meadow. It is an Other Place where anything may happen, a place seen through thick glass, whose residents, if there are residents, will not notice her passing.

Come off it, Anna, says her Inner Voice. *This is the meadow behind Dunkeld House whose every inch you love dearly and which is yours whether you like it or not.*

Anna shades her eyes with her hand. If my little Rachel is out here she is well hidden. Rachel likes to hide away from her mother's world, a world that will never win her approval. *My darling daughter.* How could such a little sober-sides come out of my belly?

Anna makes one last survey of the meadow, searching for a glint of Rachel's fiery red hair. Nothing. She turns homewards.

Even in this hot wind, Dunkeld House stands cool and apart, its stone walls and high gleaming windows, its towering oaks, ancient maples, and gigantic poplars proof against any disturbance.

My Dunkeld House.

Anna walks towards the house, the wedge of her passing through the grasses soon wiped away by the wind. It is cool on the back terrace. She rests a palm against one of four stone columns before crossing to the wide door that leads into Dunkeld House's central hallway.

Anna decides to send her cinnamon-blonde-headed, self effacing sister, Colleen, to gather the family while she herself scoops tongue soothing vanilla ice cream from the old refrigerator in the kitchen and takes out, too, the big brown crock of raspberry sauce, made from the fruit of her own raspberry patch.

"That will bring them running."

She passes down the central flagged hallway, past the many closed doors to the last room on the left, the kitchen. Colleen is there rocking in Mumma's green rocking chair.

"I couldn't find Rachel."

"She'll come in when she gets too hot." Colleen's pale oval face is bent over some embroidery. Probably for the church linen, Anna thinks wryly.

"Would you hunt up Cousin Bridget and your twins? I thought I would treat everyone to ice cream and raspberry sauce. "That will attract the whole gang. Do you want me to bring Aunt Beverly down, too? She's having a good day. She recognized Cousin Bridget, though she called her a fat bitch."

"Yes. We must have all the family."

Except for poor Mumma.

Soon the household gathers around the big kitchen table. Even dark, silent Louis, Cousin Bridget's Métis husband, has come in from the stables seeming to bring with him dappled shadows from under the maples in the front yard. Summer Wind follows him, too, stirring the green blinds on the kitchen windows. Anna sits at the head of the oval, pedestaled, walnut table. To her left Colleen's two-year-old twins are seated on either side of their mother, to prevent them squabbling. On Anna's right, her Cousin Bridget, a hefty, middle-aged, kindly-eyed nurse sits near Anna's Aunt Beverly who is beautiful but completely dotty. They hold down the tablecloth like a stone and a pebble at Louis's elbows, as if he or the table might take a notion to fly off. There are two empty chairs.

One chair is for Anna's Mumma, Faith Dunkeld, who lies within earshot in the little bedroom over the kitchen with its narrow, enclosed staircase rising from just beside the fireplace. The other chair is for Anna's daughter, little Rachel, who is still wandering somewhere on Dunkeld's grounds.

Cousin Bridget takes a mouthful of ice cream and raspberry sauce and squishes it against the insides of her round cheeks so as to miss nothing of the paradoxical, sweet-piquant flavour. The outside of her cheeks challenge the raspberries for redness. She pushes her rimless spectacles back up her knobby nose and smiles.

Anna's Inner Voice whispers, *God, how I love Bridget.*

She says, "I'll bring some dessert up to Mumma."

"I'll do it." Emma, the last occupant at table is already on her feet.

Emma is Beverly's child but she could not be less like her vacant-faced mother who has always been a flibbertigibbet. Emma moves in quietude, her dark thick hair falling across her face revealing glimpses of pale, pale skin and airforce blue eyes, the Dunkeld eyes. At fifteen she has seemingly retreated into silence. But Emma is alert always, always to the needs of others.

Anna bites her lip. How can a heart so hurt as Emma's remain so kind?

The girl says, "I'll take the ice cream up to Aunt Faith. You must be tired from the heat, Aunt Anna."

"I'm not …"

"I said I would do it." The two sets of blue eyes meet.

Anna nods. Mumma would enjoy a little visit from Emma, the quiet one. Now, if it were Anna's own child, four year old Rachel, the visit would turn into fuss and worry. The two cousins, Emma and Rachel, are opposites, the older thoughtful and vulnerable the younger abrupt and driven. As for Mumma, she lies there patiently dying as if it were the most natural thing in the world. *And isn't it, though.*

"It is hot. I wonder where that Rachel is. I hope she's wearing a hat," Anna says.

Empty eyed Beverly makes as if to get up and then flops back into her chair, her faded blonde curls bouncing. She begins to stir her treat into crimson and white spirals. She will do this until someone takes it away or coaxes her back to her room.

Anna sighs. This would embarrass Rachel if she were here. The sensitive child would be concealed in some flowered bower or other, lost in the fantastical world that provides escape from her eccentric family.

Cousin Bridget slurps up the last of her treat, smacks her stained lips and declares, "You think this is hot. Did I ever tell you about the time …?" Her dark-eyed husband, Louis, begins a slide from his chair. "You stay right where you are Louis Sauvé! … about the time …"

"Maybe I should go look for Rachel," Anna ventures.

"No you don't, Anna Dunkeld. This story is about you and all the trouble you caused when you decided to grace this world, and about your grandmother, god rest her soul, and your mother, god keep her," raising her thick eyebrows towards the ceiling.

"I know, Cousin Bridget. I caused no end of trouble coming into this world and you are never going to let me forget it." Anna always pretends to hate the story just as fervently as Bridget pretends to scold her for being born.

Bridget smiles and tilts her large head to the side.

"It was in the thirties on a torrid summer's day, a day to become known as the hottest day in Canadian history, and it was right here in Dunkeld Village in the days before the place got so high and mighty. Poor Faith was hulling raspberries with Beverly in the kitchen at the old house …

1937

Faith Dunkeld clutched her distended abdomen and leaned against the kitchen sink. Faith's younger sister-in-law, Beverly, a fidgety, fair haired girl who was steaming in a black wool swimming costume, dropped the raspberry she had been hulling.

"What is it?" she squeaked, crimson-stained fingers going to her lips.

Faith gasped, "I … I'm not feeling well. Her lovely face drained to grey and she stifled a groan. "Go … GO get someone. Hurry!" She slid to the floor, her arm, shoulder, and the side of her head bumping along the green cupboard door beneath the sink.

Beverly squealed and dashed out by the kitchen door. It banged behind her as she clattered down the stairs and across the back porch. Instead of going around by the dirt road and across the bridge over Dunkeld Creek, she shot across the back yard past the giant maple, scrabbled through Faith's garden, squashing lettuce, and leaped from stone to stone in the shallow creek that sang its way from the bush to the Ottawa River beyond the village. Thistles scratching at her, burdock snatching her bathing costume, grasshoppers leaping for safety, dust and pollen sticking to her sweat, mouth open to catch what oxygen there was, she struggled up the hill behind Cruickshank's store, stumbled across the field, and careened screeching down the rise to the swimming hole. The people in the water, coloured tea-brown during Dunkeld Creek's long journey through the surrounding forest to the Ottawa River, gaped in astonishment. A boy forgot to jump from the swing rope and hung there on the knot like a bug on fly-paper.

"Faith is having a fit!"

The women came running, bathing costumes scratching against sunburned flesh. Plump Cousin Bridget Dunkeld, a newly graduated nurse home for the summer, arrived first at Faith's grey stucco house and sent a snivelling Beverly up the road to fetch Faith's mother-in-law, Jeanne Dunkeld.

She and Bridget carried Faith, a slight burden, up the painted stairs and into her bedroom.

Jeanne almost dropped Faith's legs. "What's that on your mouth? Blood?"

Faith laughed a little hysterically. "No. It's raspberries!"

The three of them, giggling and crying, Faith stopping to bow her back in agony, Bridget trying to act like a professional nurse and then forgetting herself and ripping Faith's clothes away, Jeanne going on about having left biscuits in the oven at home, which sent them into another fit, sobered as Faith cried out.

Jeanne said, "Faith, my darling girl, the pains are coming too fast, too soon, too soon! We'll have to help you ourselves. You must be brave, child."

"Never mind being brave! Scream and yell. It'll help," said Bridget out of the depths of her two-month experience in birthing at the Pembroke General Hospital.

But little Faith didn't scream. She moaned like a trapped forest animal, and her eyes got bigger and bigger and more lost. They feared for her life. Jeanne, her blazing red hair curled crispy-wet and trailing from its old fashioned pompadour, tore down the stairs. Her youngest son, the delicate, fair-headed one called Patrick, stood at the bottom.

"Go for the doctor and send someone for Richard." Faith's tall young husband, forced by the Depression to work like a mule on the railroad.

Jeanne summoned Bridget from the bedside. The pains had stopped for the moment and little Faith lay against the pillows, semiconscious. "The new bedroom suite from Freiman's in Pembroke hasn't arrived. Faith will be mortified when the doctor gets here."

Bridget, her brown eyes expressing the opinion that Jeanne had gone mad, breathed, "I don't think she cares."

"Nevertheless." Jeanne, widow of Dunkeld Village's leading citizen, once rich, still proud and a respected teacher, church organist, mother to all, was obeyed. They crossed the road to Bridget's log house nestled among pines and carried her chest-of-drawers across the dusty surface and into Faith's house and up the stairs to the room where Faith lay whey-faced and heaving once more. It took three men to jockey the chest-of-drawers downstairs when Faith's new suite came on the train from Pembroke.

The doctor also arrived too late, pontificated, and left after consuming a bowl of raspberries. But nobody cared because Faith was alive and safe in Richard's arms.

Later that night, Jeanne stood in front of Richard while he nursed his new baby in the green rocking chair, three-year-old Colleen sitting on the mat by his feet. "You have two girls now. You'll not want her to have another, Richard."

Bridget frowned and changed the subject. "What a time. This baby better be special. I'll not let her forget the trouble she's caused."

Faith, Bridget, and Jeanne recovered. Beverly had a fainting fit and had to have camphor waved under her nose, which greatly impressed the boys from the swimming hole.

The new baby, Anna, proved small and sickly and later almost died of whooping cough, but she had intelligent blue eyes and curly brown hair, and was the bonniest baby ever born in Dunkeld Village. She was raised in a cocoon of love in a family that cared for its own and everyone else's too. And she emerged an innocent, determined butterfly into the light.

Chapter 2

THE SEWING BOX

"May I play with your sewing box, Aunt Anna?"

Tootsie, the female half of Colleen's twins, pulls at Anna's apron. She always wears a white apron in the kitchen, not because she needs one but because Mumma and Nana Jeanne used to.

Anna knows that Tootsie doesn't want her utilitarian, plastic, many-tiered sewing box with a compartment for everything, a present from Colleen. Tootsie wants the old ratty round straw box with a cover shaped like a Mexican sombrero, which Anna has, over the years, filled with round, square, beveled, center-raised, center-caved, wooden, cloth, plastic, bone, pearl, red, green, blue, brown, black, grey, white, yellow, even orange buttons; saved from old clothes, from sewing forays, from the bottom of drawers, from ancient wardrobes; and mixed with tiny conch shells, river smoothed stones, a hunk of jade her grandfather had dug from the bottom of a British Columbia creek, and a jagged piece of amethyst purchased at a rock and gem show.

"Of course, you may play with the sewing box, Tootsie. Are you taking it outside?"

The big green eyes, so much like Colleen's, gaze up placidly, not so much like Colleen. "I might sit on the stoop with Pansy." Pansy is the first in what is to be a long line of Shelties purchased by Anna as friend and comforter.

"Pansy will like that. Be sure not to misplace any of the treasures in the sewing box."

"I'll be as careful as careful can be, Aunt Anna."

"That's my girl."

Anna crosses to the window to watch the sturdy little, dark-haired child go to the stoop that leans beside the pole that holds up the clothesline. Behind her waddles the fat sable Sheltie, patient and protective. When the twins are out of sight, Anna always sends Pansy to find them and they follow her more or less obediently back to the house. The dog settles at Tootsie's feet as she settles on the stoop.

All she needs is Mrs. Dumice sitting beside her, whispers Anna's Inner Voice.

1942

Anna didn't understand why Mumma let Mrs. Dumice live in their cellar.

Sometimes on sweaty-hot days, Mrs. Dumice would come out and sit on the clothesline stoop and sew. She was an old lady with a white bun on the back of her head and combs to hold it up. Just like Anna's Nana Jeanne. But Nana Jeanne's bun was red with grey in it. Mrs. Dumice dressed like Anna's Nana, too. She had long sleeves even in summer, and she had an apron made out of sugar sacks. Nana always took her apron off when she went outside, but Mrs. Dumice didn't.

Anna asked Mumma, "Why does Mrs. Dumice have to live in our cellar?"

"It's because of the war." Lots of things were changed because of the war. There were hardly any Daddies around. Even Anna's own Daddy was gone. And there were soldiers from Petawawa everywhere on Main Street. Mumma always crossed the street when they called to her. Some of them whistled at Mumma, but Mumma said they were rude. They sounded okay to Anna. They laughed a lot.

Anna had plopped herself onto the stoop because she had crossed the creek on the stepping-stones where she wasn't supposed to go, and where she went, and got her running shoes wet. Mumma hung them on the clothesline. It was really funny to see your shoes hanging on a clothesline.

Anna was glad when Mrs. Dumice came up out of the cellar and sat on the stoop.

Mumma always said that it would be all right for Anna to talk to Mrs. Dumice if she was good. So when Anna would see the old lady sitting on the stoop, she would go and sit beside her. The stoop's wood felt warm on the back of Anna's legs and bum. She always asked Mrs. Dumice for permission before sitting down, even if it was Mumma's stoop, sort of, or maybe the landlord's. Mumma had told her that the little stucco house on Maple Street belonged to the landlord. Anyway, Mumma said Anna was to be good, so she asked permission.

"Good morning, Mrs. Dumice."

"Good morning, child." Mrs. Dumice had a scratchy voice and her hands were all corded and brown-spotted. Sometimes she had purple-black bruises on her arms, and her hair was sort of yellowed over the white.

Anna liked old people. They had lots of time to answer questions. She liked to ask questions. But she didn't ask Mrs. Dumice a lot, like she did her Nana, because Mrs. Dumice didn't talk much, or smile much.

The stoop sat near the side porch with the sleeping veranda above, and you could sit and look out at the garden and the creek beyond or at the big maple tree that Mumma loved, or you could face around and look at the house's grey stucco wall. Mrs. Dumice always looked at the wall. Anna asked her why once and she said she liked to look at the morning glories that Mumma had planted there. Anna liked them, too. They were like a bunch of pink and white and blue bells hanging on the wall. So Mrs. Dumice and Anna would sit and look at the morning glories together. Once she told Anna that the bells were magic houses that closed up at night to keep the fairies warm. Anna sneaked out at night to see if it was true. It was.

Mrs. Dumice had a basket for her sewing things. Anna thought it was really beautiful. It was made of straw but was smooth and shiny and had a lid with little shells sewn on in a pattern so they looked like shell-flowers.

Anna told Mrs. Dumice, "When I grow up, I shall have a basket just like yours for my sewing things."

Mrs. Dumice had buttons and needles and black and white and red and brown and blue thread, and darning yarn, and a red pincushion shaped like a tomato with green felt leaves. Mrs. Dumice had a thimble, too. It was just like Nana's thimble, but it was sort of dull looking, not silvery like Nana's. Anna liked to watch Mrs. Dumice push the needle's end with her finger inside the thimble. She let Anna put the thimble on her thumb once but it was too big.

Anna felt sorry for Mrs. Dumice because she had to live in a cellar. But Mrs. Dumice said that it wasn't too bad. One day, she asked Anna if she'd like to see it. Anna thought it would be scary and dark, but she didn't want to be mean to Mrs. Dumice so she went and asked Mumma.

Mumma said, "It's all right, Anna, but don't bother Mrs. Dumice too long."

It wasn't really scary. There was a sort of room like their kitchen but cold smelling and not very clean, and the windows were way up near the ceiling. There was a stove and a brown table with no oil-cloth and two chairs and a sink.

"Where's your bed, Mrs. Dumice?" She showed Anna another room, but it was scary and did look like a cellar. And it was dark, and Anna was afraid of the dark. Mumma always left the light on at night until Anna fell asleep.

There were two beds. "Who's the other bed for?"

"It's for my son, Hubert."

"I haven't seen any boy around here."

Mrs. Dumice said that her son was a big man, so Anna forgot about him for then.

The best thing of all in Mrs. Dumice's cellar was the toilet. It didn't have a room for itself but sat on a sort of box right in the room where the beds were! Anna had never seen such a thing before. She wanted to sit on it, so she asked permission. Mrs Dumice smiled, so Anna was glad she'd asked because it was nice to see the old lady smile.

Mrs. Dumice said *okay* and went out so Anna could be private. It was scary in that shadowy cellar without Mrs. Dumice there, but Anna pulled down her pants and got on the toilet and peed. She wiped herself and pulled up her pants and ran out so fast she forgot to flush the toilet. But Mrs. Dumice didn't get mad at her. Mrs. Dumice always looked sad but not mad.

Mrs. Dumice gave Anna an apple before they went out to the stoop. It was sort of wrinkly but she ate it anyway. It made her tongue sour.

One day, Mumma said, "I don't want you visiting Mrs. Dumice just now."

"Why?"

"Hubert is home."

Anna wanted to see what Hubert looked like but Mumma said, "You are not to go near him."

"Why not?"

"Because he's always drunk and brings bad women home."

Anna wondered what a bad woman looked like, but she never got to see one.

One night, she heard Hubert shouting all the way up in the bedroom that she shared with her big sister, Colleen. Anna jumped out of bed and went down to the kitchen. The stairs felt cold on her bare feet. Mumma was sitting rocking very hard in her green rocking chair.

"Mumma!"

Mumma came and scooped her into her warm arms.

"I'm scared."

"Is it the shouting?"

Anna had never before heard a man shout, though lots of mothers who weren't like Mumma shouted at their kids.

Mumma carried her to the door to the stairs that went down to the back porch door and on down to Mrs. Dumice's cellar door. "See that hook?"

"Yes."

"No one can open this door unless I unfasten that hook."

"Not even Hubert?"

Mumma nodded but her eyes were worried. Anna decided not to ask any more questions, and then maybe Mumma would forget all about Hubert.

After that, Nana Jeanne sent Uncle Patrick to sleep on their couch when Hubert came home. Daddy was far away at the war or he would have chased Hubert away, but Anna guessed Uncle Patrick was too feeble to do that. He used to live down in Pembroke, where he worked for Freiman's Department Store, but he had come home to be with Nana Jeanne because his older brothers, Daddy and Uncle Matthew, were gone to war. He now worked down at the post office on Main Street.

One day, some men came with a truck to take away Mrs. Dumice's belongings. Anna jumped up from where she'd been telling herself stories under the big maple tree and ran into the house.

"They're taking away Mrs. Dumice's stuff!"

Mumma said that Mrs. Dumice was in the hospital, but later the bad boy from up the street, Teddy Fisher, told Anna that Hubert had murdered Mrs. Dumice and that she was dead. *Murder must mean hitting.* Anna ran real quick to ask Mumma. Mumma always told the truth ... not like other big people. Mumma said that Mrs. Dumice wasn't in the hospital any more, and she was dead all right, but that she had gone to heaven to live with Jesus and Mary.

"Did Hubert murder Mrs. Dumice?"

Mumma said that Mrs. Dumice got mad about the bad women, and Hubert got drunk and hit Mrs. Dumice, and she fell and cut her head on the toilet. Mumma said that Hubert didn't really mean to hurt her. But Anna figured that anyone who hit his Mumma was almost as bad as the Germans. And she told Mumma, "I'll never hit you even if I get drunk!"

Anna didn't sit on the stoop anymore, but sometimes she went round to the side of the house and looked at the morning glories and thought about Mrs. Dumice.

She wondered if God had let Mrs. Dumice into heaven, and if He let her bring her little sewing basket.

Chapter 3

THE SUITCASE

Anna's fists clench in her apron. A sound of muffled coughing. It's coming from Mumma's room over the kitchen. Emma is there. But she's only a young girl. Anna turns from the window, takes a step towards the kitchen stairs. The choking is getting worse with heaving pauses. Anna can hear Emma's anxious voice. The bell rings. Anna is across the kitchen and up the stairs before the second ring. Mumma is sitting up in the bed leaning forward. Emma is pounding her back.

"It's all right. It's all right."

Mumma's little body is convulsing. Anna rushes over, pushes Emma aside, and slings her mother onto her stomach. "Hold her!" She crawls over the bed and grabs a wash pan from the bedside table and puts it on the floor. Then she drags, as gently as she can, her suffocating mother to the bed's edge, head hanging down. She supports her shoulders. "Now, Mumma. Now!" Faith's gags. "Hit her now!" Emma resumes her pounding. A massive convulsion as if the fragile body, no heavier than the pillows on the bed, will fracture and dissolve. A mass of phlegm like a monster birth slides from Faith's mouth. A pause. A rasping breath. "It's okay, Mumma." Anna gently turns the quivering little body and lifts it to the pillows. "Get fresh pillowcases, Emma."

"I'm all right now, Anna." Faith smiles. She smiles!

"I'll get you a clean nightie. Anna crosses to the big maple dresser, the one which replaced the dresser which Nana and Bridget carried up the stairs at the old stucco house on Maple Street so long ago, opens a drawer and chooses a pale mauve nightie. Mumma loves pretty bed things, soft and elegant coverings without frothy lace or embroidery which would irritate her desiccated skin. Anna slips off the soiled garment and substitutes the new.

"That feels so good, Anna."

Emma is back with the pillowcases. Faith smiles up at her. "You're such a good girl to your Aunt Faith."

Emma's hands are shaking. "I'll take away the …" jerking her head towards the wash pan.

Anna says, "It's all right. I'll do it later."

"I want to, Anna."

Anna looks into her niece's deep blue eyes. "All right. Thank you."

When Emma is gone, Faith accepts a little water and a quick wash of face and hands. The hands are small. Emma has manicured the nails and rubbed cream into the skin that is as dry as dead leaves. A lady's hands, and above all gentle, always gentle.

"Do you know what I was telling Emma about when this happened? I was minding her of the time you ran away when we lived on Maple Street."

Anna laughs. "I didn't do a very good job of it, did I?"

Movement on the stairs. Cousin Bridget puffs her way into the room. "I swear I don't know why you don't let us move you to a downstairs room, Faith Dunkeld. I am too fat for these stairs."

"I like to look out over the maples," Faith says.

Bridget waves her thick hand as if to disperse any tomfoolery such as gazing at treetops. She goes to Faith, moving lightly for one so big and with authority born of many years nursing. "So we had a bout, did we?"

"Anna and Emma took care of it."

"Well, I'm here now. It's time for the breathing machine."

"Oh, Bridget, Anna and I were just talking about the time …"

Bridget places her feet apart and her hands on her generously endowed hips.

Faith smiles. "All right. But you go, Anna. I don't need two of you fussing over me."

Anna bends and kisses her mother on the top of her prematurely white head. But she doesn't go back down into the kitchen. Instead she wanders into the long, wide central gallery, past eight closed doors to a small door near the end by the over-sized, many-paned window. Instead of opening into a bedroom or sitting room this door hides a narrow stair. Anna mounts to the huge top floor, once the domain of servants, now rooms full of castoffs from the house and the lives of the people who had occupied it. She goes to the end room where her things are. On an old dresser with an oval mirror frame carved with leaves, a tiny, brown cardboard suitcase rests. It is too small even for a child's clothes. Anna brushes dust from it and opens the cheap metal clasps.

Today she chooses a matchbox and opens it with a scraping noise. Inside are crumbled oak leaves, as old and brittle as memories. She and her best friend, Charlie Stuart, once wrapped such leaves in pages torn from a scribbler to make cigarettes , to be like Mumma, to smoke. Oh God.

1943

Nana Jeanne gave Anna a papier-mâché elephant with a daisy grasped in its trunk and a ladybug sitting on its head. "The elephant will remind you not to forget, because elephants never forget, you know. The daisy is to remind you never to give up hope, no matter what, and the lady-bug is to remind you to take care of people weaker than you."

> "Ladybug, ladybug fly away home
> Your house is on fire
> And your children are alone."

Anna felt a kinship with ladybugs and she knew about elephants because Nana Jeanne had shown them to her in one of her schoolteacher books. Anna really liked elephants because they were so big and strong and didn't pick on the other animals. She liked daisies, too, and often gathered a bouquet for Mumma in the field next to the pine bush-lot beside Cousin Bridget's house.

"What will you call your elephant?"

"Just Elephant."

"That's a sensible name."

"I'll keep him forever, you know."

Nana didn't smile as most grownups would. She always took seriously everything Anna said. She was strict, though. Anna didn't make messes in her house or touch ornaments unless given permission. Anna liked Nana's house because it always smelled of baking biscuits and because it had old-fashioned things in it. There was a big egg-shaped picture of Anna's grandfather, Poor Sean, with a bulgy glass over it, and a black, knobbly dresser, which contained a drawer full of ancient photographs and beautiful stuff Nana had when she was young and rich. On Nana's desk, a small, brass bust of Winston Churchill guarded a crystal inkstand with Quink Ink in it. Nana's house wasn't fancy outside, just log, but the inside was fancy.

Every Sunday afternoon, Mumma would take them over to Nana Jeanne's house. That Sunday, Jeanne and Anna were sitting quietly in the kitchen while everyone else tidied cupboards upstairs.

"Can we do some sewing, Nana?"Anna hoped to rummage in Nana Jeanne's sewing box, which was wooden and opened from the top. It also had a little drawer where buttons were kept.

Nana's chin went up. "I'm surprised at you, Anna. One never sews on a Sunday."

"Why, not?"

"Because every stitch one puts in on a Sunday must be pulled out with one's nose in Purgatory."

Anna opened her mouth to ask, "What is Purgatory?" but Nana Jeanne proved too quick for her.

"I have to write letters now and your mother and Beverly should be finished sorting quilts. Maybe you could go and check on Emma."

Emma was Aunt Beverly's and Uncle Matthew's three-year-old. Matthew was Anna's favourite uncle, though she wasn't too fond of Beverly who spent summers with Nana Jeanne to give Beverly's relatives a break while Matthew was away at war. At least that is what Anna had heard Aunt Beverly say. Anna didn't mind watching Emma who was a docile, pretty baby who never caused trouble. It was a good thing, too, because Aunt Beverly acted cranky almost all the time. Either that or she pretended to be sugar sweet, which was even more awful.

Anna's Daddy, Richard, was away at the war, too. She didn't remember him very well because he had worked on the railroad before the war, and when he came home, he always spent his time digging in the garden or splitting and piling wood. He was very tall and very handsome, and serious. Nana Jeanne said that Anna looked like him because they both had the Dunkeld nose. Uncle Matthew wasn't at all like Daddy. He did a lot of laughing and singing and teasing little girls. His breath always smelled of peppermints, and he kept a supply in his pocket, a supply he was always willing to share with his nieces. Nana Jeanne called him *Poor Matthew,* just like she called Uncle Patrick *Poor Patrick* because he had a weak heart. Anna couldn't see much wrong with Uncle Matthew. Nana never called Daddy *Poor Richard.*

Nana Jeanne cleared her throat. Anna could take a hint. She was not to bother Nana anymore today. Anna respected that. Nana was always writing letters to people like Poor Aunt so-and-so, or Dear Second Cousin so-and-so, or Great Uncle so-and-so who lived out West. Some of them were people in the pictures in the black dresser. But some letters just went to Pembroke or even to people in Dunkeld. Uncle Patrick had to mail them at the Dunkeld Post Office, though once Nana had lifted Anna so she could push a letter through the slot in the red post-box on the corner.

The Dunkeld Village workmen had put a paved road and a sidewalk like the ones downtown in front of Anna's stucco house on Maple Street, and Mumma allowed Anna to cross the street to visit Cousin Bridget and, of course, Anna's best friend, Charlie Stuart. She wasn't allowed to cross the road down the hill though or to go to Nana Jeanne's house alone.

When they got home from Nana Jeanne's, Anna asked Mumma, "Can I go play with Charlie?"

"May I."

"May I."

"If Mrs. Stuart says it's all right."

Anna sighed. Mrs. Stuart wouldn't let Charlie play with anyone but Anna and Colleen. The bad boy down the street, Teddy Fisher, said, "It's because they are Holy Rollers and Charlie's Ma is a Jigaboo." Teddy was always saying strange things like that and making nasty faces when he did.

"He is not a Holy Roller."

"Is, too. Anyway you're just as bad. You're a Catholic!"

"What are you, then?"

"I'm a Protestant, Stupid."

Anna didn't know what he was talking about but was sure she and Charlie were being insulted. "Well, you don't have shoes!" staring disdainfully at Teddy's dirty feet.

"Do, too. Only sissy's wear shoes in summer. Why don't you go play with Charlie, Sissy."

Anna, tossing her long brown ringlets which Mumma put up in rags every Saturday night after Anna's bath, looked both ways up and down Maple Street. She marched across to Charlie's house, a tall brick box with windowsills painted brown and a green hedge dividing house from street. Anna loved this hedge, thinking it mysterious and offering many nooks and crannies for secret goings-on between her and Charlie.

Anna knocked a long time before Mrs. Stuart came to the door. She was a stiff woman with long dark hair worn in rolls, brown skin and sad, black eyes. She didn't say anything, just looked at Anna.

"Can … May Charlie come out to play?"

Mrs. Stuart shook her head and was closing the door when Anna asked, "Is it true that you are a Holy Roller?" Mrs. Stuart gazed calmly at Anna for a few seconds and closed the door.

Anna backed up until she could see Charlie's bedroom window. Sometimes he would be looking out at the street when he wasn't allowed to play. There was no sign of him. Shoulders drooping, Anna went home and found Mumma in the kitchen saying her rosary beads. Anna knew she shouldn't interrupt Mumma when she was saying her beads so she went out back to find Colleen.

Her sister was playing cutout dolls in the woodshed with her best friend, Ruby Flaherty, who was in her class at school.

Anna hated Ruby on principle because Colleen preferred her company to Anna's.

"Can I play?"

"No," Colleen snapped as she carefully leaned against a log her Shirley Temple cutout doll. Shirley stared at Anna with her sugar-candy-sweet-grimace and wobbled on her chubby paper legs.

"Why not?"

"Because we don't want you," said Ruby. She was a chubby girl herself with black bangs, clever brown eyes, and no respect for Anna.

Anna bit back a retort and wheedled, "I'll bring out my ballerina colouring book and you can colour any page you want. You can use my new crayons, too."

Ruby bit her lip.

Why did *she* get to make the decisions when it was Anna's and Colleen's house? Colleen acted as limp as a snotty hankie, albeit a hankie whose face had brightened at the mention of the ballerina colouring book which, until now, had been forbidden territory.

"No," said Ruby.

Anna tightened her lips and snorted through her pointy nose. "You are a big Holy Roller, Ruby Flaherty!"

Ruby jumped to her feet. Am not, you little pig!"

"Are, too."

"Anna!" Colleen had paled in horror. "Ruby is Catholic just like us!"

"I am not a Catholic," Anna yelled. "I am going to run away and become a Holly Roller just like Charlie."

"Oh you make me sick, Anna. Go away or I'll tell Mumma."

Anna marched in the back door past Mrs. Dumice's stoop, banged through the door and up the stair and into the kitchen. Mumma prayed on oblivious to the world. Anna stalked into the cloakroom where she kept her toys, hauled out her brown, doll-sized suitcase full of doll clothes which Mumma had knitted or sewed, stuffed her doll inside and walked straight-backed out the front door and down the hill to forbidden territory.

Mumma found her there half an hour later, squatting on the curb with the dolls' suitcase under her arm. "What are you doing, Anna?"

Anna was being the Little Girl Running Away and didn't really wish to be interrupted.

"I'm running away to become a Holy Roller."

"I see. How is it that you are sitting here?"

Anna closed her eyes in disgust. "You know very well I'm not allowed to cross this road. She looked up at Mumma. Who was trying not to *laugh! I'll never forgive Mumma for this. I will do something very bad.*

At teatime, Colleen asked if Ruby could stay and Mumma said no. Now Colleen was mad. "I want my bread and butter now," she said in a bratty voice.

"Don't you have anything to add to that," Mumma asked calmly.

"No."

"Say please, Stupid," Anna said loftily.

"I'm hungry. I want my bread and butter."

"Not until you have asked for it properly."

"I'm hungry."

After a lengthy test of wills, Colleen was sent out to play with no bread and butter. Anna followed her after consuming her own tea. "I'm sorry you didn't get your tea, Colleen."

Colleen, whose green eyes were red-rimmed, put her arm around her little sister. Do you want to play cut-outs?"

"Yes, please."

That evening, Mumma finished eating supper before the girls and went out to sit on the stoop before doing the dishes. Anna suspected she was smoking cigarettes, which Nana said wasn't ladylike but which Mumma and Cousin Bridget did anyway. Anna secretly admired them for this.

"I know," Anna said. "Let's have some more potatoes. They're still hot."

Colleen got the pot because Anna wasn't allowed to take things off of the electric plate or the wood-stove. Colleen spooned out two huge piles of fluffy potatoes. Let's use lots of butter."

"Okay." Precious, rationed butter melted in golden puddles. "Let's put mustard on it." "Okay." French yellow spread on top of gold. They ate the whole pot of potatoes.

When Mumma came in, she did the dishes without a word, poured herself a cup of stale tea, sat down in her rocking chair, and asked, "Would you girls like some apple pie for dessert?"

Anna opened her eyes. She looked down at her tummy that bulged in an ugly manner. She went over to her mother. "Mumma. Can I have a rock?"

"Mumma put aside her tea and took Anna on her lap. Colleen came over and put her freckled hand on Mumma's slim pink one. "I'm sorry I didn't say please."

"That's all right, dear."

Mumma rocked. Colleen started to sing about a bluebird on a windowsill and Anna closed her eyes.

The blue eyes popped open. "Mumma. What 's a Holy Roller?"

Mumma sighed, "Oh, Anna."

It was Charlie Stuart who finally explained. They were sitting behind the hedge playing with Charlie's metal cars. Charlie had a sort of pointy head and not much neck. He was shaped like a roly-poly toy. But Charlie was always calm and Charlie was smart. None of the other kids in the neighbourhood were smart like Charlie and Anna. The girls were especially boring. They were always worrying about dirtying their shoes or their dresses. If they had nice toys like dollhouses, they wouldn't let anyone play with them. One stupid girl had pulled down her bloomers and dared the other girls to kiss her bum. Everyone squealed and shrieked in horror. A disgusted Anna had marched up and kissed the fat pink bum. It was like kissing a rubber ball. So what was the drama all about?

Charlie would never act like that. When asked, he said calmly, "They were probably just curious and they like to make things dirty."

"May I ask you a question, Charlie?"

"Of course."

"Are you a Holy Roller?"

Charlie smiled. "Yes, I guess I am."

"What does it mean?"

Charlie thought about this. "Well, you're a Catholic. You pray to statues and stuff and you have all kinds of fancy stuff in your church, and priests and nuns and rosary beads …"

"So what's wrong with that?"

"Nothing. My mother says that you and your sister are the most decent kids on the street, and she likes your Mumma.

"Anyway. Lots of people say that in my church we go crazy and roll around in the aisles."

"Do you?"

"Of course not. But we do get very euphoric sometimes."

"Euphoric?"

"I'm not sure what it means, but it's a good word, isn't it?"

"Yes. When I go to school and am allowed to attend the Children's Mass, I shall be euphoric, too."

"Would you like to make some cigarettes?" Charlie asked.

"You mean like Mumma and Cousin Bridget smoke that nobody is supposed to know about? Where would you get cigarettes?"

"Colleen, Ruby, and I pooled our allowance and bought some at Cruickshank's store. We said they were for your Mumma."

"Did you smoke them?"

"No. We hid them under the hedge, but it rained all day and the cigarettes were ruined. We were probably being punished for our sins. Anyway. We made some out of oak leaves. Want to try?"

"Sure."

They gathered oak leaves from Mrs. Cruickshank's back yard, tore them up and laboriously made two rather fat cigarettes. Charlie had matches in a little tin box he always kept in his pocket, just in case he should get lost in Baker's Bush beyond the swimming hole and have to survive the night. Not that he was yet allowed to go to Baker's Bush, but nevertheless … They smoked the autumn-smelling cigarettes, choking and sputtering and almost setting fire to the hedge. Anna did not think it a good experience, but she didn't throw up like Charlie.

Just before she staggered off home, she said, "I don't care if you are a Holy Roller, Charlie, I like you the best."

Charlie smiled. When Charlie smiled, his whole face lit up. "I like you, too, Anna."

That summer of Anna's sixth year held many other *stories.* Mumma let her put pieces in her big people's picture puzzle with the mountain scene and told her she was a remarkable child when she got a lot of pieces. Teddy Fisher saw Mrs. Dumice's ghost peeking out from behind Mumma's maple tree. Ruby and Anna ate a whole cabbage right out of Mr. Flaherty's cabbage patch and nobody got mad. Colleen, Ruby, and Anna made mud pies and cakes to feed their collection of dolls. Anna had received a little table and chairs, some china dishes, and some tin pots and pans for her sixth birthday. She had, of course, to share them with Colleen and Ruby. The mud cakes were things of beauty decorated with dandelions and acorns and rosehips from Mumma's yellow rose bush that grew beside the front porch. Anna discovered that by using two different kinds of dirt, one could make a light brown and a dark brown batter and swirl them together to make a beautiful pattern.

That evening Teddy crept onto Anna's porch and stole the table and chairs and hid them in his back shed. Anna went and told his mother and his mother took a switch and grabbed Teddy's arm and beat and beat him all over his skinny body. There were long red marks with blood in them on his legs.

Anna ran home, screaming, "No! No! Teddy's mother is murdering him!" She wept unconsoled in Mumma's arms.

"Why would she do that, Mumma? Why?"

"She doesn't know what else to do, Anna."

Mumma would slap Anna's wrist when she was really bad and call her a little *wrig*. And sometimes, she would say, "If you don't behave, I shall have to spank you." This meant, "You have gone too far." But Mumma never actually did it.

But Anna thought she would really get that spanking when she stole a cat.

It started out as a wonderful story. Nana Jeanne had an old, cranky cat who stayed out all night and scratched children who tried to pick her up. When Anna asked for a cat, Mumma got very pale and said, *No*, in a voice that meant there would be no argument. Anna told Nana Jeanne and Nana Jeanne told her that, when Mumma was a baby, a cat had sat on her face while she slept in her cradle. She had been terrified of cats ever since.

They had been out picking pussy willows near Baker's Bush. Sometimes Nana liked to take long walks with Anna and tells her stories about the Dunkeld family before they got poor and about Anna's grandfather, *Poor Sean*. That day when they got back to Nana Jeanne's kitchen, she put the pussy willows in a basket behind the wood-stove.

"Why are you doing that, Nana?"

"Because when one puts pussy willows in a warm place, they will sometimes turn into kittens."

Anna's whole body tingled. "Promise?"

Oh yes, it will really happen. But, the kittens must stay here, you understand."

Some weeks later, Nana Jeanne showed Anna the basket, and in it snuggled and mewed and wiggled two kittens, a black one like Nana's cranky cat and a yellow one. This miracle, of course, meant that Colleen had to take Anna daily to look at the kittens. One day they entered Nana's kitchen to find her gone. She was probably over at the church playing the organ.

The words were out of her mouth before Anna could squeeze them back. "Let's take the black kitten home."

"Are you crazy. You know Mumma is afraid of cats."

I know but listen, listen. We can hide it under the front porch. There's a hole behind the rosebush. It could never get out through the slats. Mumma would never know.

"And how would we feed it?"

"I'll feed it."

They took the kitten and stuffed it under the front porch, that is, Anna did. Colleen marched off declaring that she would have nothing to do with stealing.

That afternoon, Mumma sent Anna and Colleen to Cruickshank's Store for a loaf of bread. "I know," Anna said. "We can pick a hole in the end of the bread, and hollow out a space and keep all the bits to feed Blackie,"referring to the stolen kitten. "Mumma will never notice the hole."

Having completed the excavation, they secreted the pile of bread bits under the porch. The kitten sniffed it curiously and began to mew.

"Stop mewing, you stupid cat. Mumma will hear you."

Mumma said nothing about the hole in the bread, but when Anna sneaked out to check the kitten the next morning, she found a saucer of milk under the porch. Anna ran squealing over to Charlie. "The Fairies brought milk for my cat!" she shouted.

"Charlie frowned. "I doubt fairies had anything to do with it."

"What then?"

"I don't know."

Anna thought a lot about this that night and in the morning, she put the kitten in her doll carriage and brought it back to Nana, even if she wasn't allowed to walk over there herself.

Nana said, "Oh, that's where that kitten got to. It went to your house for a visit."

"Yes, Nana."

"Odd thing for it to do."

"We are going to hell, you know." Colleen whispered that night.

"What's hell?" Anna asked.

Chapter 4

SCHOOL

Today, Anna has volunteered to drive Emma to school. And it is for a reason. At fourteen with hormones beginning to boil and bubble, Emma is still a seemingly self-contained, placid child. God knows where she gets it from. Anna glances at her. Thick dark hair falls forward hiding Emma's face. She is plumpish and pale skinned, probably doesn't have the faintest idea how beautiful she is.

"I used to go to the Convent you know, though it certainly doesn't show now," Anna says.

Emma turns, her airforce blue eyes twinkling. "You and Grandma and Great Grandma and god knows how many cousins and aunts."

"We had to wear those heavy black uniforms with hard collars and cuffs, too." Anna reaches over to pat Emma's hand.

Emma looks down at her cuffed wrists. "And you loved it. Grandma told me how you rebelled when the nuns wanted to change your uniform. I personally think a skirt and blouse and blazer would be far more practical."

Anna laughs. "You're not fooling me. You'd give your eye teeth to go the Protestant high school."

"And go straight to hell when I die?"

"They're not still teaching that, are they?" Anna groans.

"The nuns hate it but the priests are so afraid of losing their almighty status that the Baltimore Catechism still rules, though the cooler nuns make it quite clear what they think.

"Tell me how you beat the nuns on the uniform thing."

Anna sighs. "I was so damned innocent. A bunch of new nuns were making all kinds of changes. I'd always been a leader and the girls did pretty much what I wanted, but the nuns were leery of me. I picked two other seniors and went to the Sister St. Anthony to complain about the uniform change. It was stopped."

"I'll bet they were scared of you."

Such a thing had never occurred to Anna. "They did decide not to allow a student's council that year because I would be president and probably cause them a lot of trouble, though I didn't realize that until years later. I also wouldn't have got the stole of honour that they present at graduation to an outstanding pupil if it hadn't been for Sister St. Anthony."

"She's Principal now."

"You're lucky."

"She hates my guts."

Anna wonders why but knows better than to ask.

Anna has always thought of Emma as a baby sister and she now considers Emma a talented, dreamy girl who wants only to be loved. Anna remembers how she adored the child when she was scarcely big enough to lift her. She was Anna's number one audience for stories, and the two of them would sit for hours under Mumma's maple while Anna told Emma tales about Borrowers and elves and good witches. God knows that having a mother like Beverly, the child had enough misery to contend with.

As if reading her mind, a thing she is quite capable of doing, Emma asks, "What did the specialist in Ottawa say about Mother?"

Anna believes in truth. "There's no hope. Beverly may take a very long time to deteriorate and her worst character traits will probably become exaggerated. As her short-term memory continues to fail, she will need more and more supervision."

Emma is silent as Anna knew she would be.

They reached the Convent, still as anachronistic in its brick glory as ever, and beloved.

"Say hello to Sister St. Anthony for me."

Emma smiles her enigmatic smile.

It's a while before Anna starts the car. She is seeing the ghost of herself, a little girl, wandering hallowed halls when priests were gods and nuns their handmaidens.

1943

Anna was going to school.

"Hurry, Mumma. We'll be late!"

"Stop worrying, Anna. Worry is like sweeping up smoke."

Mumma slipped on Anna's cotton waist, which buttoned down the back, pinned garters to it and then pulled up long, brown, ribbed stockings on her sturdy legs and fastened them to the garters. Then came the black bloomers, which Nana had made, and finally, the uniform! Anna was too young to wear the hard celluloid collar and cuffs with gold collar studs and mother of pearl cufflinks, but she got to wear a lace collar and little lace cuffs sewed to her sleeves. And glories of glories, at her neck bloomed a huge, black, silk bow, the final touch to the uniform of a real Convent Girl attending The Convent of Our Lady of Snows.

Mumma began to put a little white sweater over all this finery. "No, Mumma. I don't need it!"

Mumma gave Anna's ringlets a final pat, tied a smaller black bow on the plumpest one, and took Anna to the kitchen table where a new brown school-bag lay beside two scribblers, a fat red pencil, a pink eraser, and a Reader. Anna already knew this book off-by-heart.

See Mother. See Father. See Baby. See Puff. See Spot. See Puff run. See Spot run …

"Now don't let on you can read," Colleen said, "or you'll make Sister Marie cross."

"Don't worry. I'll act just like the other kids."

"You must do exactly what Sister Marie says, Anna." Mumma looked and sounded serious. "Colleen will bring you to the school-yard, but you must line up with the little ones when Sister Marie comes out and rings her bell. And remember to curtsey when you meet a nun in the halls, and don't talk back, and don't pick your nose, and don't be bossy with the other children, and …" Mumma was a Convent graduate, as was Nana Jeanne.

"Oh, Mumma! I'm going to school!"

Mumma smiled and gave her a big hug. "Now promise me you will wait for Colleen at lunch-time. She will walk you home at first."

"Mumma, I shall remember everything and will be the most perfect girl in the whole class."

Mumma just raised her eyebrows and sighed. She stood on the porch waving as they went down the hill.

It was a mile-long walk to school, down Maple Street, past the Railroad Baron's mansion with its own park; under the railroad trestle; across the wooden bridge over Dunkeld Creek; across the big metal bridge over the Anishinabe River; past a lot of brick, stucco, and clapboard houses; past the Protestant Grade School; past the white Catholic Church with its steeple, stained-glass windows and cross; and finally to the brick building whose statue of Our Lady of Snows stood guard under the topmost eave. The Convent was also defended by a green lattice fence, a stand of oak trees and a dirt playground with a dilapidated pair of basketball nets, the only sign that things as secondary as physical education went on there.

Off in a corner was the Our Lady of Lourdes grotto which separated the Convent from the Boys' Continuation School across the street and from the much larger Separate School. These three schools were the biggest in the Village, numerical superiority going to the Catholics and monetary superiority to the Protestants. In the Ottawa Valley, every town and village, no matter how large or small, had the same set-up, a Protestant Grade School, a Catholic Grade School; at least three churches, Catholic, Baptist and either Lutheran, Presbyterian or Anglican; and in the larger villages a Protestant High School and a Catholic High School. Only the tiniest hamlets had to send their children to town after grade eight. Dunkeld, though less than a quarter the size of Pembroke, boasted both a Convent and a private Boy's School.

I'm going to play with the big girls," said Colleen dropping Anna's hand which she had clutched painfully all the way from Maple Street. "You go and make friends with the baby class."

"I'm not a baby."

"You are here. And don't talk to the big girls unless they talk to you."

Anna was to learn that Senior Girls had attained the lofty pinnacle of Grade Thirteen and a strict pecking order was in place. However, the Seniors were unfailingly kind and condescending to the babies, as long as said babies followed the unwritten rules.

A group of girls Anna's size were playing *Ring around the Rosy* under the biggest oak which shaded both the west side of the convent and the church. Another straggly group stood around looking left out and lonely. One of these girls peeked from behind the oak's trunk. Anna went to her.

"Hello. My name is Anna. What's your name?"

Head with black bow tied to a hank of straight clay-coloured hair, uniform a trifle big. The head bent down. A little voice whispered, "Bitsy."

"Why aren't you playing, Bitsy?"

Silence.

Anna looked around. "Come on," she said loudly to the left-out crowd. "We're gonna play *On a Mountain*. I'll be the lady." Timorous figures gathered round. Anna climbed on a rock under the oak; the rest joined hands and began to circle her, singing,

> *On a Mountain*
> *Stands a lady*
> *Who she is I do not know*
> *All she wears is gold and silver*
> *All she needs is a fine old beau*

The circle stopped singing, stood silent. Anna's clear voice fluted,

> *I call in Bitsy, Dear Bitsy, Dear Bitsy*
> *I call in Bitsy, before I gang ahae*

Bitsy stumbled forward, head down, cheeks flaming. Anna jumped from the rock and handed Bitsy up. The circle turned and sang.

A fairy bell tinkled. Ten black bows swung toward the sound. On a little porch leading to the big girl's cloakroom stood the tiniest lady Anna had ever seen. She was a nun. A Grey Nun of the Immaculate Conception, looking like something out of an old story with her long brown dress covered to the waist by a sleeveless black domino, head wrapped in starched white linen outlined by a stiff, black face-frame shaped like an upside down *W* with bow-like protuberances at the neck. A graceful, black silk veil hung down her back. Around her neck hung a silver cross and a black cincture bisected her skirt, vertically. Her tiny hand held a brass bell, which tinkled once more. The babies knew by some magical prescience that the summons was for them. They gathered in a cluster at the foot of the steps to the big girls' cloakroom.

Sister Marie spoke. Her voice sounded muted and musical like her bell. She did not smile but somehow Anna knew that she was gentle.

"Grade Ones will line up one behind the other according to size, smallest in front." Awkward scrimmaging. Anna found herself midway in line. Bitsy was up front. A beautiful blonde girl stood in front of Anna.

"What's your name?" Anna whispered.

"Charlotte," was the whispered reply.

Sister Marie's diminutive head cocked sideways like the chickadee she resembled. "There will be absolutely no talking in line or anywhere else in the halls or upon the stairs. The foremost girl will follow me. The rest will follow her." And up the steps and through the big girls' cloakroom they went, past the music hall to the base of the stairs. Sister Marie halted. Scrambled halt behind her. She turned. "If we should meet a Sister coming down the stairs, you shall halt and wait until she reaches the bottom. You shall mount the stairs on the side where the wall is. There will be no need to curtsey to the Sisters when you are in line. However, should you meet a Sister when on your own, you must pause and curtsey. "

A small voice, "I don't know how to curtsey, Sister."

"You shall be instructed. And from now on, there will be no talking in line. Should you have a question, save it for the classroom." A pause. "You reply, *Yes, Sister.*"

The errant voice whispered, "Yes, Sister."

Up the stairs they went, past a wonderful blue and white statue of Mary and down a long dark hall with a window at the end. Anna was to learn that progress in Our Lady of Snows began at the very end and on the left side of this hall, in Baby Class, and ended in Grade Thirteen on the right. Big girls with mounds of books clutched to their swelling bosoms straggled down the hall on the right side. They were so beautiful and powerful that Anna swallowed tears.

Baby class smelled of chalk, furniture oil, and floor wax. Each little girl was assigned a desk with a wooden top, an inkwell, never to be used, and wrought iron legs painted black and shined to distraction. Sister Marie's desk was small which befitted her. To one side stood a huge sheaf of pictures on a stand. It had been flipped to show the first picture, a brightly coloured Jesus with children gathered at his feet. The walls were decorated with a brown crucifix and lined by long blackboards with narrow shelves holding white chalk and felt erasers. Above the blackboards marched the ABC's, both small and capital, and numbers from one to twenty.

At Sister Marie's instruction, Anna slid her school bag, scribblers, and book inside her desk. She placed her fat red pencil and her pink eraser in the groove provided near the inkwell.

"Good morning, girls," said Sister Marie. "You stand at the side of your desk and reply, "Good morning, Sister."

Anna and the rest leaped to their feet, "Good morning, Sister!"

"Please be seated."

They squirmed into their desks. *My very own desk.* Anna sat as straight as a Shirley Temple cutout doll.

"My name is Sister Marie. Now, how many of you know how to make the Sign of the Cross and say the Hail Mary? Raise your hand if you know. Anna's hand shot into the air like a struck peggy.

"Good. Now for the rest, touch your forehead with your right hand and say after me, In the name of the Father … fold your hands, bow your heads, and repeat after me … Hail Mary, full of grace …"

Clouds of sainthood circling her head, Anna murmured the prayer, being careful not to rush ahead of the rest. Happiness tingled in her toes, crept up her legs and shot up to her brain where it radiated star warmth. *I am in school!*

Anna noticed a dark-skinned girl with baking-chocolate eyes like Charlie's mother. The girl had a calm dignity in class and answered all questions quietly and correctly. After the Hail Mary, Sister Marie had each girl stand and give her name which she printed on the blackboard. This girl's name was Theresa Sauvé and there was no doubt she was Indian. The beautiful blonde Charlotte Green seemed pretty smart, too, though not as clever as Theresa.

Anna bit her lip. She might even be as smart as me. A dizzying thought struck. Now I shall have real best friends, and Bitsy, too, of course.

At recess she learned that Charlotte lived in the West End of the village and Theresa over the restaurant on Main Street where her mother worked as a waitress.

"Who's your daddy?" Anna asked Charlotte.

"He got killed in the war."

Anna felt anger rise in her gullet. "That's crazy! You're telling a lie."

"I am not." Charlotte's lovely morning-glory-blue eyes flooded.

Immediately contrite, Anna put her arm around her new friend's shoulder. "I'm sorry. I didn't think daddies could get killed." She looked around for Theresa and Bitsy. Theresa was standing beside the big rock under the oak and Bitsy was sitting on the rock. Anna took Charlotte's hand and led her over to them. "Come and play."

Theresa turned to Bitsy. "Come on." Bitsy hung her head.

"Come on, Bitsy!" Anna said. All three girls stood looking down at Bitsy whose head hung lower. "Leave her," Anna said. "She'll come when she feels better." Theresa looked Anna in the eye. Anna tried to read what she was thinking but couldn't.

"I'll stay here," said Theresa.

Shrieks and squeals emanated from near the green fence where the rest of the Grade Ones were playing *Run Sheep Run.* "Okay," said Anna, beckoned Charlotte and trotted to join the fun.

Colleen seized Anna's hand. "You've been dawdling. We'll be late back from lunch." She dragged Anna whose short legs pumped like the needle in Nana's sewing machine. When they got to the Protestant School, Colleen walked all the way around the schoolyard on the sidewalk.

"Why don't we cut across?"

"We can't, Stupid." "Why?"

"Just because. Now hurry up."

A voice from the schoolyard called, "Hey where ya goin', Convent Girls. Stuck up!"

"Don't look," Colleen ordered.

"Dirty stuck-up Catholics." Laughter and jeers. Anna's pumping legs stopped. "Come ON, ANNA!"

"But they …"

"They are just stupid Protestants. They don't know any better. Ignore them."

The next morning, Anna had an emergency. She raised her hand. Sister Marie said, "Yes, Anna?"

"Please, Sister, I have to go to the bathroom."

"Did you go at home?"

"Yes, Sister."

Sister Marie pushed aside her domino and withdrew a tiny silver watch on a chain. Anna's eyes rounded. "All right, we shall go as a class. Line up girls, first row first, please." Down the hall they marched, down the stairs, past the music hall … but here they swung left and descended another stairs into the bowels of the earth. At the bottom they saw a double row of hooks on the wall, some closed doors, and a dark empty rectangle. The rectangle swallowed Sister Marie and presently a dim light showed. "You will come in here two at a time. The rest stay in line and be silent." She let Anna go first with a red-haired girl behind her. Not only Dark lived in there but Anna could hear a big old furnace rattling and whooshing. Maybe Hubert Dumice was hiding behind the furnace. Happily they did not go as far as the furnace room. Two open doors with hooks on them, one step up and a really tall toilet with a stool in front of it.

Anna thought of Mrs. Dumice.

"Do you need help, Anna?"

Was she going to stay and watch her pee? Surely nuns didn't go to the bathroom. "No, Sister." But if she went away, Anna would be alone in the growling dark, or almost dark anyway.

"How about you, Jane?"

"All right, you may close the doors if you wish. I shall stand here. And Sister Marie turned her back, took out a very big black rosary and began mumbling her beads just like Mumma.

One day, Colleen, who was learning to play the piano, had to stay for practice at noon hour. Mumma had asked Anna, "Do you know your way home?"

"Of course I do."

"Well, just this once, you may come on your own. I have asked Mrs. Sloane if Bitsy could walk with you." It turned out that Bitsy lived just down the hill and up a side-street from Anna's house. "Bitsy's older sister has a cold, so you'll take good care of Bitsy, won't you?"

"I shall guard her," Anna declared.

And she did. Except when they reached the Protestant School. Many of the Protestant children had gulped their lunches and were already in the yard. A game of softball was in progress. Now, there was a beaten path right through the schoolyard, tromped down by the townspeople on their way to Main Street, when the children were in class. This path cut off the long sidewalk route which Colleen always made Anna take. Anna paused and then set one black shoe on the path. Bitsy gasped and pulled back.

"Come on, Bitsy."

"No." A remarkably stubborn little snort from Bitsy.

"I'm going across the schoolyard."

"No."

She dropped Bitsy's trembling hand. "Okay. You go around and I'll meet you at the other end. Then head high, back straight, Anna strode down the path directly onto the ball-diamond. She longed to close here eyes. A terrible silence gripped the schoolyard. Anna could hear whispering. On she went expecting any minute a softball to strike her dead. She squished her shoulder blades together and marched forward. No gang of boys rushed her. No Big Girl came to pull her ringlets. No teacher ran screaming from the school. Anna marched on amid deadly silence. Just as her toe reached for the sidewalk at the end of the path, a boy's voice called, "Way to go, brat." She whirled. It was the bad boy from up her street, Teddy Fisher. She raised her chin, shook her ringlets, grabbed Bitsy, who had run all the way around the schoolyard on the sidewalk, and went on her way.

The next spring, the Protestants put up a chain-link fence around their schoolyard. Anna was convinced that they did it just to keep her out.

The friendship between Bitsy and Anna flourished. After that first day, Anna never again broke up the softball game, so Bitsy agreed to walk home with her. Colleen swanned off with Ruby Flaherty, walking so fast that the little ones couldn't keep up, to Anna's secret delight. For Anna spent the time telling Bitsy stories. Anna told her wide-eyed new friend every tale anyone had ever told her and then began to make up new ones, in which a little girl with ringlets emerged triumphant from every adventure every imagined. Bitsy was either enthralled or was just content to let Anna talk.

One day, Bitsy didn't come to school. Anna said to Theresa, "Would you walk a little way with me?"

"I could go around the block, if I hurry home after that."

Delight surged through Anna. It was the first mark of open friendship Theresa had shown though she was always friendly.

Full of vinegar with this success, Anna said, "Let's go out the side gate and walk by the Boy's School."

A moment's hesitation. "If you want."

They had almost passed the boys, whose habit was to line the sidewalk and torment the girls from the Separate School, when a voice asked, "What ya doin' with the Jigaboo?"

The air sank away out of Anna's chest. She whirled. Lots of boys but narry a one looking at them. Theresa continued to stroll along, her dark head held high. They went in silence to the corner. Anna wanted to say something but, for once, could find no words. Finally, she said, "Thanks for walking with me, Theresa."

"Why don't you call me Tess. My family does."

"If you don't mind, I'll call you Theresa at school. It sounds so important."

"Okay."

"See you at school tomorrow, Tess."

"See you."

Chapter 5

RAPTURE

During that wonderful first year of school, Anna discovered Mary Queen of the May, St. Anthony, and Christ the King and was captivated for life.

The chapel at Our Lady of Snows Convent was a wondrous place. Hushed, private, with nunnish prayer-murmurs, childish voices raised in song, and the creak of wooden pews, and altar rails burnished to a state of heavenly shine. The white and gold altar stood raised under a niched dome where hovered Mary, lovely, resplendent in azure and white robes, a loving all-forgiving mother with cherubim at her feet and the muscular Angels, Gabriel and Raphael, guarding her sides. Below hung the red sacristy lamp whose glow reminded worshippers when Jesus was present in the form of the sacred host. The spicy scent of incense hung on the air. To either side of the altar stood stately statues of St. Anne, Mary's own saintly mother after whom Anna had been named; St. Anthony, protector of children; The Sacred Heart, Father and Guide; and Mary herself as a modest young girl.

When Anna knelt among the babies in the very front pews, she knew that she had found all that was good and kind and beautiful.

Add to this the procession through the school during the Month of Our Mother, the blessed and beautiful May. All the girls, from the tallest, prettiest Grade Thirteener to little Bitsy, donned white veils fastened with wreaths of spring flowers, wound white rosaries through their fingers, and joined the procession. In the lead glided the head girl carrying Blessed Mary's silken banner on the end of a pole, a banner from which streamed long white satin ribands held by four proud Grade Two's. The Principal, tall Sister Mary Catherine, led the way and the nuns brought up the rear, murmuring their Aves.

They proceeded first to the grotto in the yard and, wonder of wonders, water flowed from the rocks, replica of the blessed waters of Lourdes. Lilac bouquets graced every terraced stone. Afterwards, the procession wound its way through the music hall with its polished pianos and down the stairs to the kitchens, where the kitchen nuns, two red-cheeked Irish nuns who smiled a lot and were seldom seen above ground stood, heads bowed beside their huge black stoves, and on into the little boarders' playroom and the dining room. Anna's head turned from side to side in wonder. They traversed the refectory on the main floor where the big girl boarders did their homework and filled their leisure time in the evenings. Up, up they went to the boarders' dormitories where each virginal bed hid behind white curtains. Of course, they did not go into the nuns' quarters but they passed the door.

And all through this, the children's choir sang wonderful hymns about Mary.

"'Tis the month of our Mother
The blessed and beautiful day
When our lips and our spirits
Are glowing with love and with praise…"
And
"On this day, O beautiful Mother
On this day, we give thee our love
Near thee Madonna, fondly we hover
Trusting thy gentle care to prove
On this day we ask to share
Dearest Mother thy sweet care
Aid us ere our feet astray
Wander from thy guiding way…"

Tears stung Anna's eyes. Mary was like Mumma but sacred on top of it.

Ruby Flaherty brought Anna down to earth on the way home that day.

"Sister Boniface told us that if we want to be Christians we have to be willing to be martyrs."

"What's a martyr?" Anna didn't trust Ruby but she sometimes was the purveyor of interesting information.

"In the olden days, lots of Christians got killed because they wouldn't become pagans."

"What's a pagan?"

"You don't know anything, Anna Dunkeld."

"So tell me."

Anna could see that Ruby wasn't just showing off, her face looked wan and her brown eyes rounded with fear. Ruby gulped. "A pagan adored statues of bulls and things instead of Jesus. And if Christians didn't do it, too, they would cut out their hearts or burn them up or feed them to lions."

"What did the Christians do?" asked Anna, interested now.

"They just let them and then they went to heaven."

"Well there, you see. They got to go to heaven, so it's not so bad."

"I hope I never meet any pagans."

"I hope I do. They can cut off my head if they like. I shall not kneel in front of any bull."

This soldierly promise was further strengthened when Anna attended the Feasts of Christ the King and of the Holy Childhood in the church where the kids from all the Catholic schools gathered in the presence of their parents to form another, even longer procession that wound through the streets of Dunkeld past little shrines raised on Catholic lawns. The Convent girls wore their uniforms and white veils but the other kids, of course, just wore their best clothes. The Bishop came up from Pembroke to lead them and all the priests and nuns were out. Most of the Protestants stayed politely indoors but a few lined the sidewalks in silence, suitably awed, Anna thought.

Back inside the church, big boys in cardboard armour painted silver carried in banners and all the kids sang:

> *There's a crimson banner flying.*
> *There's a bloodstained flag unfurled*
> *For the Knights of Christ are marching*
> *To the conquest of the world*
> *There's a great white general leading*
> *Who is bearing all the brunt*
> *Bravely holding front line trenches*
> *On a far off eastern front*
> *Won't you answer, Yes I'm ready."*
> *When they call the muster roll*
> *Won't you join the Holy Childhood*

And win the world for God.
And
An army of Youth
Flying the Standard of Truth
We're fighting for Christ the Lord
Heads lifted high
Catholic Action our cry
And the cross our only sword
On earth's battlefield
Never advantage we'll yield
As dauntlessly on we swing
Comrades True
Dare and Do
'Neath the Queen's white and blue
For our flag, for our Faith
For Christ the King.

Christ lifts his hand
The King commands
His challenge, "Come and follow Me."
From every side
With eager stride
We join in the ranks of victory
Let foemen lurk and laggards shirk
We throw our fortune with the Lord
Mary's Son, may Thy will be done
Here on Earth as it is above

An army…

Someday, Anna would be a missionary and would conquer the world with all its evil and make everyone good. She might even save Charlie Stuart and some other Protestants.

Chapter 6

FAITH'S STORY

The Christmas of their second year at Dunkeld House, Louis carries Faith down from her bedroom to the library. He has felled a large spruce, and Anna and the children have decorated it with old glass balls and bells and Santas and angels and reindeer and snowflakes and the dozens of ornaments Faith has collected or the children have made over the years. The room is dark except for firelight and a few candles flickering, and when Faith is ensconced on the couch, Bridget turns on the tree lights.

Anna looks around at her family. Mumma's face is shining as if the Christ Child Himself had come to visit. Rachel and Emma and the twins sit on the hearth rug near her. Louis is enjoying a celebratory drink of rye, something he seldom does. The Aunts occupy armchairs on either side of the gigantic fireplace with its carved gargoyles. Christmas music plays softly on the record player that Anna has given Emma.

God almighty. How idyllic it all looks. If only …

Colleen comes in. Even in the muted lighting, Anna can see that she has been crying. Surely she doesn't miss that brute of a husband.

Faith takes a sip of the sherry Bridget has allowed her and says, "My dear family. If only Richard and Patrick and Jeanne were here."

"They are here, Mumma," Anna says because she knows that's what Faith wants her to say.

"Shall I tell you a Christmas story?" Faith asks the twins.

"Yes!" Jimmy, the male half of Colleen's twins, shouts.

Anna knows what is coming. The story will be altered for the twins and Rachel's sake but Anna relives it all.

Faith takes a deep breath. "It was 1943 I think and Anna was only six years old …"

41

1943

The *Eaton's* truck had just pulled away when Anna trudged up the front verandah steps of the grey stucco house on Maple Street. The boxes were piled in the center of the kitchen floor. Faith rushed to the front door.

What could she do? She couldn't leave Anna out there in the cold while she hid the parcels!

She pulled open the inner vestibule door just as Anna opened the storm door. Blue eyes peered at Faith above a red scarf covering nose and mouth. A little frost circle glistened on the red.

You're half frozen, honey!" Faith pulled her youngest inside, snatched off her mitts and held the little fingers in her own warm hands. "Why didn't you wait for Colleen?"

"I know the way and the snowdrifts aren't too big. And I walked on the sidewalk."

"Colleen will be looking all over for you. Who helped you with your leggings and galoshes?"

"Sister Marie."

The frosted little face was already turning pink. Faith steeled herself. Anna would believe her. The child could be a real handful, but she trusted everyone completely.

"Look, honey. Are you warm now?"

"Yes."

"Do you think that you could go to Nana's for me?"

The blue eyes lit with drama. Anna loved to walk the two blocks to Nana's, especially before Christmas time when Nana would give her hard little cookies with multi-coloured sprinkles and little balls of silver candy on them. And because she was the baby in the family, she loved even more being entrusted with a *job!*

Faith gave her a hug.

"I know the way to Nana's!" Before Anna had started school, she and Faith had gone every Monday morning to Nana Jeanne's house. Jeanne had an electric wringer washer, an almost unobtainable luxury during wartime, and Uncle Patrick had his brother, Matthew's old car from before the war. On Sunday night, Patrick would pick up Faith's dirty laundry and take it to Nana Jeanne's house. In the morning, Faith and Anna would go to do the washing. The machine had to be filled with warm water heated on the summer kitchen cook-stove at Nana's, but when the washing was done, Anna had the special job of putting a pail under the little tap at the base of the green washer and turning the tap. She would watch breathlessly as the gray, sink-smelly water poured into the pail and turn off the tap just in the nick of time before overflow. This always made her feel very grown up and responsible. However, since starting school, she had missed out on this weekly adventure. She was pulled back from memory by Faith's voice.

"You tell Nana that I want Uncle Patrick to bring back the laundry tonight. Can you remember that?"

"I can remember. I'm a big girl."

Back on went the mittens and up over the pointy nose went the red scarf. Faith watched her go down the icy path. "Please, St. Theresa, let Jeanne realize why I sent the child with such a fool message."

Faith closed the door, fled up the steps and across the small living room. She paused and looked over at the photograph of uniformed Richard smiling at her from the top of the piano. How many things he must have done without to send the extra money for what was in those *Eaton's* boxes.

"Come home safe," she breathed as she always did when passing the photograph.

She entered the kitchen. It smelled pleasantly of baking fruitcake and felt toasty warm just as it always did when the girls got home from school. It was a long walk to the Convent and a difficult one for Colleen who had to haul her baby sister over the snowdrifts. The wood in the stove crackled.

"I'll have to get in some more slabs."

Faith's glance paused on the open door of the corner cupboard where she kept her baking things. How did they ever manage to get up there and find those raisins? Lucky that Mother and Bridget could give me some for the cake, with rationing and all. I want Richard to have that cake for Christmas. She saw the *Eaton's* boxes. There were so many of them! Where could she possibly hide them until Patrick got there?

"Hurry," she told herself. "You have only a few minutes." She crossed to the door to the back stairs and unbolted it. She opened the door and peered down the stairs that led to the wartime basement apartment, which their landlord had foisted on them. She hated going down there, always fearing that the ghost of Mrs. Dumice would be sitting on a kitchen chair beneath the high cellar window.

The boxes were so heavy! But she had to get them out of the way. Tiny Faith bit her lip as her fingers jammed against the railing. She was just puffing up the stairs for a third time when she heard the front door. It was Colleen. The child was in tears, hopping and wiggling desperately.

"What's wrong?" Faith flew to her.

Colleen wailed, "I couldn't find her. I looked everywhere. Sister Marie said that she left with the other kids. And it's snowing!" Colleen's eyes were as crimson as her always rosy cheeks, and her coppery blonde curls stuck in spirals to her sweaty forehead.

She must have run all the way home. "It's all right. Anna walked home by herself. She's over at Nana's."

"That little brat! I thought she crossed the ice on the Anishinabe River and got drowned … and I peed my pants!"

Preparing for Christmas was difficult and lonely with Richard gone, but Faith managed it with Patrick to help. Poor Patrick, refused by all three armed services because of his weak heart and reviled by those who knew no better. One woman had pinned a white feather on his lapel and Nana Jeanne said that he had disappeared into his room for days. Richard's older brother, Matthew, had also gone to war, leaving Jeanne alone with Patrick and Matthew's skittish young wife, Beverly, and little Emma. Patrick had cut down the Christmas tree on a wood lot on the old Dunkeld estate, and had decorated the tree with red, blue, green, and yellow lights. He also helped Faith put the gifts together when she opened the boxes to find a jumble of parts! Somehow she found time to knit some doll's clothes and dress up one of Anna's old dolls and pack it in a box for Emma. Though there were hard times in Jeanne's household, Matthew wouldn't send home extra pay like Richard did and Patrick didn't make much, and now Jeanne had Beverly and her child, Emma, to look after. *Faith hoped Matthew wasn't drinking again.* Emma was too young to realize she was getting Anna's old doll. Anna would have to understand somehow when told that she must not tell Emma that her new doll looked just like the one that Faith had given away to the poor children.

Christmas Eve came at last.

Faith tucked her girls into bed. They shared the bed under the clothes-hooks in the bedroom above the kitchen where the chimney would keep them warm for the first few hours of sleep, after which their young bodies would do the rest. Colleen's green eyes were round with excitement.

"Did you go to the bathroom?"

"Yes, Mumma. Do you think that Santa will be able to find us?" Colleen asked, biting at her lower lip.

"Of course he will. Why do you ask?"

"Because of the war."

"Santa Claus could find anything," said Anna solemnly.

Faith smoothed Colleen's hair. "You just go to sleep now and remember to say your prayers. And remember not to eat any candy or drink water in the morning. You have to go to communion."

"I won't." Colleen, who was wallowing in a religious phase, promised.

"I don't have to go to communion," declared Anna. Then guiltily, "I guess I won't eat any candy though. Well maybe one chocolate."

"You got that chocolate egg at Easter," said Colleen.

"So did you."

"Not a big one like that priest brought you." The priest in question had been a hero of Anna's since his first visit to Grade One at the Convent. He always had in his pocket three little red rubber balls which he could make disappear and then find in a child's ear or even once under a huffy Sister Marie's veil. Though there were only two priests in the village, Anna had only recently connected him with the priest who had come to Anna's house at Easter in a shiny black car to make a *Parish Visit*. He had presented Anna with a large chocolate egg with candied roses all over it. Anna had tried to ask him a lot of questions but he only wanted to talk to Mumma.

"Well you sat on it!" Anna yelled, referring to the Easter egg.

"It was a' accident!" said Colleen, lip quivering.

Anna relented. "It tasted okay anyway."

"Enough talking," Faith said and hugged each in turn.

"Will you leave the light on?" asked Anna, as she did every night.

"Yes, I'll leave the light on."

The kitchen clock chimed midnight. Faith was rocking in her green chair, putting the final stitches in a pair of diamond patterned socks which she was knitting for Patrick, when she heard the noise on the stair. Hubert Dumice? No. Hubert was long gone, and anyway the noise came from the other stairs, which led from their kitchen to the upper floor. Anna peered around the doorjamb.

Thank God the lights were off in the living room. "What are you doing up?"

"I heard Santa in the chimney."

"You did?"

"Yes and I'm scared he's gonna get burned up!"

Faith went to her and put her arms around her. The brown ringlets were in a tangle and the child did look genuinely upset.

"Don't worry. Santa is a spirit, the Spirit of Christmas. He can't get burned up."

"Sort of like a ghost?"

"No."

"Like a'nangel?"

"Yes, more like an angel."

"He doesn't really come down the chimney, does he?"

"Not really."

"He could walk right through a locked door, couldn't he?"

"Yes, even a locked door."

"Did he come yet?"

"He can't come while we are awake. You scoot back to bed, and I'll be up in a minute." But Faith could see that there was one more question bubbling inside the inquisitive child. It popped out.

"Do you think that there will be a banana in the toe of my stocking?"

God-in-heaven, what next? No. I don't think so." There might be an orange if you are very good.

"When Daddy comes back from the war, will I get to eat a banana?"

"Yes. Daddy will get you lots of bananas."

"What do they taste like?"

"Go to bed now, Anna."

When Faith had tucked her back in beside the sleeping Colleen, she extracted a solemn promise that Anna would not go back downstairs on her own. Then she went back down herself, banked the fire in the kitchen stove, closed the dampers, checked the door hook and just before going up, went into the living room and plugged in the Christmas tree lights.

The multi-coloured lights traced the worry lines on her fine-boned, pointy-chinned face. The two doll carriages were there, a big maroon one, and a little blue one. The two miniature highchairs stood side by side. The first held a doll with china green eyes and reddish blonde hair, just like Colleen's. The second had curly brown hair.

Anna will say that it's *naturally* curly just like hers.

Faith looked at the photograph on the piano. "Merry Christmas, Richard," she said, just before putting out the lights and going up to her empty bed.

Anna has other memories of that idyllic Christmas.

Uncle Patrick gave Anna and Colleen season's ice skating tickets to the ancient clapboard arena on Maple Street. Every small town in the Ottawa Valley had its own arena from which graduated generation after generation of hockey players, all hoping to play for the Pembroke Lumber Kings. The girls were destined to be *fancy-skaters*. So Anna got bob-skates and Colleen inherited an old pair of white tube skates from Cousin Bridget. They trotted proudly down the hill, skates hanging from their shoulders with Mumma walking behind, stumbling a little in her high-heeled boots with black fur around the top.

"You can't come in with us," Colleen wailed when they reached the battered door of the arena. "Everyone will think we're babies."

Anna frowned. "Who will put on my skates?"

"Probably that Charlie Stuart," Colleen said.

"Charlie doesn't have any skates! He won't even be here!" Anna wailed.

"I'll put on your stupid skates!" Colleen gave her a little push.

Mumma looked dubious but she said, "Well, if you help Anna. And you are to hold her hand all the time on the ice and make sure no one bumps into her. And do not talk to soldiers, do you understand?"

"Why not?" Anna really wanted to know.

"Just don't!"

"We promise, Mumma." Colleen grabbed Anna's hand.

"All right then. And you must come directly home when skating is finished."

"Yes, Mumma."

The Arena seemed huge with a roof almost to the sky. In fact, one could see the sky through hundreds of cracks in the roof. The wooden floors were chewed from generations of skated feet, and the girls' dressing room had benches along the wall, a tiny toilet room, and smelled of wet wood. You could see your breath floating translucent white in the air despite the small black stove which occupied the center of the dressing room. Big ladies and little girls wearing heavy jackets of red, brown, black, navy and white; wool leggings and rainbowed toques and mitts made from yarn ends, sat side by side on the benches, leaning over to lace and tie their skates. Some of the ladies and big girls had fancy skates, black, white, or brown, with high tops and little hook buttons and no tubes in the blades. Some day Anna would have skates like that.

Colleen had already put on her skates while Anna gawped about. "Sit down!"

Anna climbed on to the bench. Her feet swung free in the air. Colleen said, "Slant your foot down, Stupid." Anna did her best but every time Colleen tried to fasten one set of straps around her boot, the other set got tangled.

A lady with a purple, tasseled tam said, "Here, stand up child and I'll put on your skates." Anna watched the kind lady expertly attach to her boots the bob-skates.

"I could do that," Anna said.

"I'm sure you could," said the lady and walked away on blades, the epitome of beauty and kindness.

Walking on the bob-skates wasn't hard but Colleen seemed to be having trouble with the tube skates. "Take my hand and we can balance each other," Anna said.

They had wobbled out to the rink boards, stepped carefully over the lintel at the opening when Colleen fell with a thump on her bottom. Anna helped her up and watched her stumble away, arms flailing. Anna looked down at her bob-skates. She pushed her legs. Nothing happened. I'm not gliding! She tried walking which proved easy enough in the slush near the boards, but unsatisfactory. Why don't I slide along like everyone else? Around her gods and goddesses whirled and flew on invisible wings. I don't know what to do. Anna felt a lump forming in her throat. Then St. Anthony slid to a stop beside her. He didn't have on his brown dress but he had on a soldier's uniform and his round face looked kindly and his grey eyes twinkled. He was St. Anthony in disguise.

"What's wrong, little one? First time skating?"

"Yes, St …mister. I want to go fast and these dumb skates won't even move."

He bent down and grasped her waist with two big hands, just like Daddy's, and swung her up to his shoulder. In no time, they were soaring and whooshing around and around and around. Anna laughed out loud. She saw Colleen flash by. So this was skating. A Strauss waltz floated from the loudspeakers and Anna swayed to the music.

When they stopped, Anna forgot herself and said, "Thank you, St. Anthony."

The soldier grinned. "I've got a little girl far away in my home out West." Anna didn't think St. Anthony had little girls of his own but she smiled politely. "You practice real hard and never mind being slow. Everyone is slow at first. Next year St. Nicholas will bring you tube skates."

"I certainly hope so," said Anna and went pushing and scraping off, one hand on the boards the other stuck out.

"I'm telling Mumma you talked to a soldier."

"You're just jealous. Anyway, it wasn't a soldier. It was St. Anthony."

"Sometimes I think you are strange, Anna."

"Well, I certainly hope so. "

It wasn't long before Anna realized that Bitsy was circling the ice with her big sister, and soon they were stumbling along holding hands.

"There's Teddy Fisher behind the boards," Bitsy said. Bitsy was afraid of Teddy. Nevertheless, Anna dragged her over there.

"Why aren't you skating, Teddy?"

"Don't wanna." A year passed before Anna realized that Teddy didn't own skates or a season's ticket and had probably sneaked into the arena without paying.

"Wanna come search for coins?" Teddy had sort of a lost look in his slanted hazel eyes so Anna replied, "Sure, how?"

"You have to take off your skates." He pointed at the once red and blue and white wooden benches that lined the edge of the rink in three tiers. "When people jump around at the hockey games, coins fall out of their pockets and if you search under the benches, you can find some."

"Don't want to," declared Bitsy.

"Well, I do," Anna said.

Soon she and Teddy were crawling about under the stands among old gum wrappers, moldy bits of hot dog, used Kleenex tissues, and dirty single mitts. Teddy seemed a different creature down here. He talked quite pleasantly to Anna, and when he found a quarter and a dime and she found nothing, he gave her the dime.

"Thanks, Teddy. Why aren't you always nice?" Teddy's thin face reddened and he looked like he wanted to hit Anna.

"What would you know about it, you dirty little Catholic." Teddy scuttled away like a startled crab, banging his head on one of the stand supports.

Anna wanted to call after him but didn't know what to say.

Later Anna stumbled back onto the ice and was slip-sliding along when she noticed a man watching her from behind the boards. He was small for a man. And skinny. He wore a black knitted cap and a dirty overcoat that was too big for him. His hair hung down over his collar and when he grinned at Anna, his teeth were yellow and brown. He squinted at her through rheumy eyes.

A voice behind her said, "Better not talk to Old Man Logan. He eats little brats like you for breakfast." It was Teddy. He had sneaked onto the ice without skates, running and sliding and endangering himself and everyone else.

"You're just trying to scare me, Teddy Fisher!"

"Suit yourself, brat."

Anna looked again at the man. He was sidling along the boards. A rink rat skated over to him and said something. The man scuttled away.

I wonder is he a bad man? Anna tossed her head and wound her way stubbornly around the ice.

The very next week a boy called Douglas White who lived next door to Nana Jeanne invited Colleen to a sleigh ride at the Holly Roller Church.

"She can't go if I can't go!" Anna shouted.

"You're just jealous because you weren't invited, big baby."

"Am not."

"Are, too."

"Now girls." Mumma was baking raisin pie and her hands were white and sticky with dough. The wonderful fruity smell of boiling raisins permeated the kitchen. Anna had been happily making her own little pie out of a ball of dough and some strawberry jam when Colleen made her announcement.

"Anyway, you told me that Sister Bonaventure said that we would go to hell if we went into a Protestant church."

Colleen's red-gold eyebrows rose and her green eyes got all swimmy. "Mumma!"

Mumma sighed. "Now enough of that. Colleen will not be going into the body of the church. The hot chocolate and cookies will be served in the church basement. And Douglas is a nice little boy."

Chocolate? Cookies? Anna abandoned her pie, wiped her hands on her stomach and ran into the cloakroom. In no time, she had struggled into a coat and galoshes and shot out the front door, across the road and knocked on Charlie Stuart's door.

Mrs. Stuart answered. Anna jumped right into her request. "Mrs. Stuart. There's a sleigh ride with hot chocolate and everything at the Holy Roller Church and Colleen is going and nobody asked me. I don't think they'd mind if I went even if I am a Catholic and Charlie could take me and you could ask the ladies and I would be very polite and not call anybody a dirty Holy Roller, so will you please?"

Anna could swear that Mrs. Stuart smiled. But everyone knew that Mrs. Stuart never smiled.

"Charlie would be delighted to take you, Anna."

Ann forgot herself and hugged Mrs. Stuart's leg getting pie dough all over her dress.

Colleen and Anna had a grand time at the Holy Roller Church. The man who drove the sleigh had horses with bells on, and the Holy Roller ladies were all round and smiley and kept asking Anna if she would like another cookie.

For some reason, Anna thought of Teddy. The voice in her head said, From now on, I am not going to listen to anyone about people, even Mumma and Nana Jeanne. Even the Bishop!"

Chapter 7

GO IN PEACE

Anna looks about her at the many books she has salvaged and scavenged for the Dunkeld House library. It is an eclectic collection, everything from the books Santa gave her as a child such as *Little Women and Little Black Sambo* to her dark Russian novels that made her cry when she first read them.

In grade eight she wrote her first book report and included the information that she had read twenty-four books that month. Sister St. Ambrose kept her in after class for lying and she had to clean the blackboard brushes by banging them with a ruler on the iron fire escape, a job she rather liked. The task finished, Anna told Sister St. Ambrose in verbose detail all about the twenty-four books and was let go early. In high school, Anna discovered boys and Emilie Loring, her mother's favourite romance writer. The stories Anna told herself then became love stories with her as heroine. Real boys she avoided like the beach in polio season. She got fat from eating chips and chocolate bars and reading love stories in her room while all the other girls were out jiving around in poodle skirts and see-through blouses. Naturally she still wrote school cheers, half the school newspaper, letters to anyone who'd let her. She read movie magazines, too, and had a secret, magic love affair with Rock Hudson. Writing was easy for her. It was like breathing. She won an essay contest with a thing she wrote in ten minutes. There was no competition.

However, in a convent school where Shakespeare and Dickens ranked right after God, Mary, Joseph, St. Anthony, St. Theresa, and the Bishop, she was not a real writer. She simply had a knack. She was different like the girls who aced mathematics were different.

"Nevertheless, I was going to be a writer, another Dickens … and all I am is …"

1944

In Grade Two, Anna discovered the Public Library and sin.

There weren't many Grade Ones that year, so Sister Marie went off to wherever nuns go and Sister St. Timothy invaded the Grade One's room where she placed the babies on one side and the Grade Twos on the other away from the windows. Anna got to keep her desk though. It safeguarded a brand new reader, which Anna had read in its entirety the night before, and an Arithmetic book.

Fat Sister St. Timothy had very red cheeks and very round spectacles. She bustled a lot and when she entered the room, a cool wind seemed to blow in with her. She smelled of humbugs and lye soap. She also talked very loudly though she was strict about the girls talking in the hall or on the stairs.

"I shall have to punish Grade Twos if they break the rules." She blinked her big, round, royal blue eyes and looked worried.

Anna knew all about punishment. Bitsy's big brother had told her that in the Separate School the strap was used often and mercilessly, especially on the boys. Anna had also heard the big girls talking in their cloakroom about Sister St. Ambrose who was elderly and stooped and feared, and who taught the grade seven and eights, and strapped you if you got an arithmetic problem wrong or if you laughed in class or even if she didn't like the way you looked at her. However, the idea that Anna herself might be punished was just too silly to contemplate. It was just another story.

Sister Timothy was saying, "This year you shall make your first Confession and your First Communion. This means that you shall be learning the Act of Contrition so you can confess your sins.

Anna's hand shot up. "What's a sin, Sister?"

Sister St. Timothy didn't scold her for asking too many questions like Sister Marie would have done. "Well Anna, a sin is when one does something bad like telling a lie or hurting another or forgetting to be kind to those less fortunate than oneself. Can anyone tell Anna about other sins?"

Charlotte's hand went up. "Stealing, Sister." Anna thought of the black kitten.

"Getting your clothes dirty," another girl said.

Sister explained that getting clothes dirty was not really a sin but one shouldn't do it anyway, especially one's uniform. "Can anyone tell me what Confession is?"

Tess proved an expert on this. It seemed you went into a box and told a priest about your sins and said an Act of Contrition and got a penance and were sorry and promised not ever to do it again and then your soul was clean and white just like Mary's and you could go to heaven. Anna wondered where Tess had learned all this and asked her in the school-yard.

"My big brother told me. "

"What grade is he in?"

"Grade five."

Just like Colleen. That sneaky devil. She never told me she went to Confession. I'll bet she has lots of sins to confess. Imagine how bad she would be if she didn't go to confession. Anna wondered if she herself had committed any big sins. She lied sometimes but that was only stories, usually told to Bitsy who didn't really count. She was mean sometimes and shouted a lot. Was shouting a sin? She wondered if she would get as her confessor the priest who gave her Easter Eggs. If so, he probably would never give her another one. She decided that she would follow Colleen to confession and find out what it was all about.

The very next Saturday, she told Mumma she was going to play with Bitsy. She guessed was a lie but it is for a good cause. She followed Ruby Flaherty and Colleen to the white church beside the Convent.

She had forgotten her black tam so she put her handkerchief on her head. It had a bit of snot in it but God wouldn't mind. Surely He was far too busy to worry about such things. The confessionals were fancy carved boxes with a door in the middle and green curtains on either side from under which sinners' feet stuck out. Anna identified Colleen's brown shoes with a hole in the sole and crept up close to the confessional trying to look like a sinner standing in line. She could hear Colleen clearly, the priest not so clearly. She crept closer.

"… and it's been two weeks since my last confession. Father I told a lie to my best friend. I ran away and hid on my little sister because she wanted to play with me and I …" Colleen sounded really scared. Maybe she had murdered somebody. Anna leaned closer. The words rushed from Colleen" … and I committed a sin against purity."

Silence, except for Anna's breathing through her mouth. She often did this because her nose was narrow. She held her breath.

The priest asked, "Do you know what purity is, child?"

"No, Father."

"Then why on earth do you confess a sin against it?"

"I don't know, Father."

"You must not ever do this again. Confessing sins you have not committed is a sin in itself. Now say a good act of Contrition, and for your penance say three Hail Mary's and one Our Father." He started droning in Latin just like at Sunday Mass. Anna walked quickly out of the church. She wouldn't confess something she never did. That stupid Colleen. She committed a sin right in the confessional. Anna didn't make that mistake. When her turn came to confess, she had a formula ready. There was no use counting up sins like stitches on an embroidery hoop, she would confess three lies and three fightings with her sister every second week. The sins would even out and God would be happy and she would go to heaven.

First Communion was another question. Anna could hardly wait to receive Jesus into her heart. She practiced faithfully with a round piece of paper on her tongue. Mumma made for her a beautiful silky white dress and got her white stockings and white shoes. Anna made Mumma take a snapshot of her beside the yellow rose bush. She wore her veil and a wreath of tiny pearls and white felt flowers. Nana gave her a white prayer book with dozens of wonderful coloured pictures of Jesus, Mary, and the Saints in it, and Daddy sent her a pearl rosary from England. Anna didn't yet know how to say the rosary but she would keep it forever. On the big day, she walked slowly up the church isle with her class and knelt to receive the sacred host. It stuck a little on her tongue but she rolled it off and swallowed it. She felt like an electric light had been turned on in her chest and that it shone all around her. Surely now she would be good.

A week later she got the strap. She and Charlotte and Tess had not only been talking but giggling on the stairs, and when Sister St. Timothy remonstrated, they couldn't stop giggling. A terrible silence later descended upon the classroom as Sister St. Timothy said in a trembly voice, "You shall have to be punished, all three of you." Charlotte started to cry. "Come to the front of the class, now." Tess went forward first, quiet, dignified. Anna marched after her. *This was surely the most exciting and scary story she had ever been in.* Sister St. Timothy went to her desk and picked up a wooden ruler. She said, "Hold out your hand now." Anna stood first in line. The ruler came down, not very hard. Anna's eyes widened. She pulled her hand away. She looked up at Sister St. Timothy. *Sister St. Timothy had tears in her big round eyes!* "Hold out your other hand." It didn't even hurt, just stung a little. Ruby Flaherty hurt her more when she pinched her. Then it was Charlotte's turn and Tess's. Charlotte cried. Tess did not. Soon the whole class was blubbering, and Sister Timothy had to tell them to fold their arms on their desks and lay their heads there. She read them a story about a little girl who was so angelic that Jesus Himself came to get her when she died.

"Maybe Saint Anthony will come for us," Anna whispered to Tess.

Her fingers were to hurt a lot more when she started music lessons. Anna loved the music hall with its four polished pianos each played by a girl sitting straight-backed, feet and knees together, arms straight out, and fingers curled. But it wasn't easy to become one of these girls. However, if Colleen could do it, Anna knew she could. That is, until she met Sister St. Luke, her piano teacher. Sister St. Luke was the real life sister of the priest who gave Anna Easter eggs and she was beautiful. Her face was creamy and even, like the ladies in The Lady's Home Journal. Her fingers were long and smelled of hand lotion. It must have been natural to her because Anna knew that nuns were not allowed to use lotions lest they commit the sin of vanity. Sister St. Luke always had a box of chocolates on her desk, probably an offering from the chocolate distributing brother who was also beautiful.

Anna tried very hard to please Sister St. Luke. She sat up straight. She curled her fingers just so. She hardly ever made a mistake. At first, Sister St. Luke liked her, complimented her on her curly hair, and let her sing the words of the first pieces she learned.

> *Here we go*
> *Up a road*
> *To a birthday Party*
> *And*
> *Dolly dear, sandman's here*
> *You will soon be sleeping.*

But Sister St. Luke proved fickle and though she laughed and hugged Anna on some days, on others she whacked Anna on her fingers with a black Eversharp Pencil if she made a mistake. This punishment did hurt and Anna's fingers ached for a long time on Sister St. Luke's bad days. Anna simply retreated into herself and, while waiting to return upstairs, wrapped her stinging hands around the hot water pipe which stood outside the music room door. She laughed inside when, after a particularly painful lesson, Sister

St. Luke gave her a chocolate and sent her out of the music hall through Sister Margaret Mary's empty room.

One day, the Eversharp Pencil came into use many times, and Anna lost hold of her inner safety and wept. Suddenly the door to Sister St. Luke's room banged open and a white-faced Colleen stood there. She looked absolutely terrified but also completely furious.

"If you ever hit my baby sister again, I shall tell Sister Margaret Mary on you!" she choked out.

She grabbed Anna, pulled her off the piano stool and snarled, "Come on!"

Outside, she yelled at Anna, "Now see what you've done! All the nuns will hate me now."

Sister St. Luke never hit Anna again. And Anna never got another Easter egg from the pretty priest. Old Father Duke made the parish visits to Maple Street from then on, and he made Mumma and Anna and Colleen kneel for his blessing. He acted cranky and gruff and the hem of his cassock was always dusty and he stunk of pipe tobacco. Anna liked him a lot. She started to go to him for confession, and one day heard him say as he closed the door over the screen between him and the sinner, "Will this never end?"

In no time, summer holidays began and Mumma took Anna with her to the Public Library.

"Now you must be very quiet in the library or Miss McKrachen will be cross. She is the librarian and she looks after the books and lends them out to those with library cards."

Anna had never been so excited. Mumma often brought children's books home from the library, took Anna on her knee and read to her. Here was another world just like Anna's own story world but infinitely more thrilling and with characters who did brave and wonderful things. Now Anna would get to see the place where these amazing books were kept inviolate under the ward-ship of Miss McKrachen, known all over the village as a dragon of great rectitude and an infinite fount of knowledge about *books!*

The library was built of reddish-orange brick and one approached it up seven cement steps bordered by two columns of funky smelling marigolds looking for all the world like little yellow and russet cadets. In order to climb the steps, Anna had to hold Mumma's hand and stretch her legs until she thought her garters would break. Inside the library near the door loomed a high mahogany desk and above it towered Miss McKrachen herself, a tall, cadaverous woman with grey hair in a bun behind her head, a grey dress with a narrow lace collar and cameo at her throat. Her spectacles didn't have any arms and clung to her humped nose with only the help of a droopy black string.

"Good afternoon, Mrs. Dunkeld," whispered Miss McKrachen. "And who would this be?"

"I'm Anna," before Mumma could stop her.

"Anna wants to become a member of the library," Mumma said humbly.

Miss McKrachen removed her spectacles and stared at Anna. "And why do you wish to become a member of my library, Anna Dunkeld?"

"Because I love books."

Miss McKrachen straightened her back even more, if that were possible, and regarded Anna once more. "Then we shall have to give you access to them, shall we not?"

"Yes, please, Miss."

When Miss McKrachen handed Anna her library card, she gave her the passport to a land of stories, better stories than Anna could make up, places of safety and wonder and thrills and weeping and miracles and horses and mountains and …

"Of course, you must confine yourself to the children's book section and obey all the rules and get your books back in time or there shall be a … fine." Miss McKrachen spat the word out as if it scalded her tongue.

Anna promised solemnly to obey, that is, she would only sneak peeks at the Adult section now and again.

Everybody in Dunkeld Village feared and sneered at Miss McKrachen, everybody, that is, except Anna and Faith Dunkeld.

One day, Bitsy got tired of listening to her stories and Anna decided that maybe she could print them on paper. So she got out her lined scribbler and her fat graphite pencil with the red handle and wrote a story, spelling the words any old which way but knowing the story off by heart anyway. This led to the forming of the Busy Bee Society, Anna's literary group. Mumma had been reading to her *Anne of Green Gables*. The members of the Society were to meet every Saturday morning at ten o'clock under Mumma's maple tree. They were each to write or tell a story. Bitsy joined, of course, and Charlie, and for a while Ruby and Colleen. As it turned out, Anna was the only one who ever produced a story. They had three meetings and folded. However, Anna was certain this was the beginning of a wonderful future.

Chapter 8

THE PICNIC BASKET

Anna is polishing Nana's silver cutlery when she hears Louis's old Ford stop outside. She glances at the kitchen clock. It is only just three o'clock and Louis doesn't usually come home from work until five. Louis has a winter job at the tiny old glove *factory* on the western edge of the village where his native skills at working deerskin can be utilized and the man who runs things leaves him to himself. In summer, Louis takes care of the grounds of Dunkeld House, does maintenance, and helps Anna with the gardening. His wife Bridget pays for the coal in winter and Louis keeps the furnace going.

"What can he be doing home so early?"

Anna comes to her feet and drops the polishing rag when Louis comes in and she realizes that he has the twins mittened hands clutched in his big paws and that Tootsie and Jimmy are upset. Tootsie has been crying and there is snot all over her face.

"What is it?"

"They were talking to someone down by the gate. I ran him off."

Anna drops to her knees in front of the children, her insides twisting. "Don't be frightened now. Were you talking with a stranger?"

"Yes but …" Jimmy starts.

"Jimmy made me." Tootsie is crying again.

Anna looks up at Louis. "Did they … ? Did he …?"

"No. It was Old Man Logan."

A terrible anger seizes Anna. "I thought that old bast…, he was in prison."

"They let him out again.

Thank god Rachel wasn't with them but safe in her room playing school. Traitorous thought but why is it Rachel seems more vulnerable than other children and has to be treated with kid gloves?

Bridget comes in. "What's wrong?"

"Nothing. These children have been very foolish and have been talking to a stranger. Louis was kind enough to bring them into the house. Would you make some hot chocolate for them?"

"Of course." Bridget begins to remove soggy snowsuits and boots. Louis turns to go. Anna crosses to him and takes his arm, a liberty he would not allow many people.

"Thank you, Louis."

He nods and goes back outside. Anna knows she will not see him again until dinner time. She leaves the children to Bridget. She will have to talk to Colleen about this and Colleen will get all in a fluster. But before she does that she must do something else.

She goes into the library where she can be private and dials a number on the telephone. A gruff male voice says, "Constable Duffy here."

When Anna hangs up, she puts a knuckle between her teeth and bites hard on it. Memories flood in.

1945

Anna loved to go to Baker's Bush. Then she could be the little girl with natural curls going on a picnic. Often she took her friend Bitsy along because Bitsy would do anything Anna asked, and this was handy when being the little girl with natural curls going on a picnic. But Bitsy's mother sometimes wouldn't let her go out and play. This happened and Anna accepted it, though her own Mumma never refused her permission to play.

"I need a basket."

"You'll find a peach basket in the cellar."

A rectangular peach basket with its fruity smell did not satisfy Anna's idea of a picnic basket which should be round, woven of straw, have a smooth handle, a red chequered picnic cloth, little dishes, and a bottle of lemonade. That's what children had in books. Nevertheless, Anna climbed down to the cellar and found the dusty peach basket on a shelf where Mrs. Dumice used to keep her dishes. The dishes were gone, and the stove, and the table, and the two chairs. Even the toilet was gone from the second cellar. Anna cleaned the basket with Mumma's dust cloth, the one Anna used to wipe the carved legs of Nana's piano, and once more trotted into Mumma's green-painted kitchen.

"What can I have for my lunch?"

Mumma sat on the green rocking chair saying her beads. Sometimes she knelt backwards on the chair with her legs and black-laced shoes sticking out and her arms on the chair-back. She should have looked uncomfortable on those occasions, but she only looked dreamy.

"There are lots of Nana's apples in the ice-box."

"Can I make a san'wich?"

"Yes."

Anna took the bread from the bread-box and the knife with teeth from the drawer. She put them on the oilcloth-covered table and climbed on a green-painted chair. She cut the bread. The slice started out all right but got thick at the bottom. She knew Mumma was watching but also that she would say nothing. Anna turned the bread upside down and cut another thick-bottomed slice. Now they would fit together in one fat sandwich. Uhoh, she'd forgotten the breadboard, and a neat little black line sliced through the yellow flowers on the oilcloth. She rubbed at it with her finger.

Anna found some sliced tomato in the icebox and put it on the bread. She didn't take any butter. Anna didn't like the feel of butter in her mouth, but she liked how tomatoes made bread all wet and cool. She almost took a piece of pie, but saw there was only one. Mumma would need that. Instead, she took some of Nana's scabby apples. She wouldn't eat them, but they looked all right in the picnic basket.

"What are you going to drink?"

"Water?"

"Take a nickel from my purse and buy a pop at Cruickshank's store."

Anna got the black patent-leathered purse from the hall table drawer, opened it, and took out the cloth change-purse. Once she had stolen a dime from Mumma's purse. Mumma knew. Mumma knew everything. Bitsy would have got a licking for that. Mumma had just told Anna to put the dime back but she had a sad look in her eyes. Anna would never, ever steal another thing from anybody.

"How far are you going?"

"To Baker's Bush."

"Just as far as the rock?"

Anna picked up the picnic basket. The nickel already felt sweaty in her palm. She would go into the Bush. That's where the mayflowers were and the fairies.

"There are often men in Baker's Bush." Mumma had stopped rocking, and the white rosary beads lay still in her hand.

She meant the kind of men who walked the railroad track or came to the back door for food sometimes. Their eyes never met yours. Anna had never seen a man in Baker's Bush. She did not answer her mother.

The big rock felt warm against her bum. She felt glad she hadn't worn trousers but a cotton dress with a pattern of sprigged blue flowers. Nana had made the dress with bloomers to match. Anna loved the way the bloomers matched the dress, even if Colleen said that Nana put old elastic in the waistbands. This was probably true. Once Anna's bloomers had fallen down right around her ankles in the middle of the sidewalk. Colleen had been so upset that she ran away. Anna kicked off the bloomers and folded them neatly over her arm. Her bum felt sort of open to the breeze, but nobody saw as she was careful not to bend over until she got home. Anyway, it felt really good sitting on the warm rock.

She examined her arm to see if freckles were appearing. Anna could never catch them growing, but they would be there the next morning. The field smelled hot. She raised her head, squinted. Bees buzzed around tall yellow weeds and purple weeds. Anna used to pick weeds for Mumma when she was little, but now she picked mayflowers. She took a red and white dishcloth from the peach basket and got out the tomato sandwich. It was wrapped in waxed paper taken from yesterday's bread, paper with blue writing on it. Clean wax paper from the store or even a white lace napkin would have been nicer. Anna shrugged and bit into the sandwich. Her mouth was hungry, but her stomach wasn't. The sandwich tasted cool and squishy. She found the metal opener and opened her lemon-lime pop. She drank a bit and put the metal top on again. The wrinkly parts at the edge bit into her fingers. She placed the bottle at the rock's base where the grass hid it, so the pop couldn't leak into her basket. After some thought, she wrapped the apples and the bottle opener in the dishcloth and hid them there, too. Now she could put mayflowers in the basket.

Anna threw the basket over the wire fence at the edge of Baker's Bush and lifted the centre wire to make an opening. She climbed through. Her skirt caught on the wire, but there were no barbs so it came away easily. She retrieved the basket and stood gazing into the trees. Shade hovered in there and dark loomed high up among the tree branches. Young looking plants blanketed the ground. Anna stepped confidently through them, their feathery green fingers touching her ankles above her socks. She searched for the telltale leaves of poison ivy and found none. Baker's Bush enfolded her in cool. She closed her eyes and snuffled the sharp plant smells. She licked her lips. *The fairies are here today.* She let the fairies guide her among the trees. Anna felt a glowy feeling in her chest when she found the first mayflower. It was three-petalled and white, and its leaves spread like delicate, heart-shaped tongues. Anna told herself a story about a little girl who got lost in the woods and was rescued by tree fairies. She saw three red mayflowers but picked only one because there were never many red. When she found the jack-in-the-pulpit, she just knelt beside it and ran a finger along its rubbery petals. The nuns at the Convent had said that if you picked a jack-in-the-pulpit, it never grew again.

When Anna reached the road that cut Baker's Bush in two, she paused. She never wandered beyond this road anymore because the trees on the other side had white trunks, and the sun shone through the branches so much that no mayflowers grew there. No woods fairies played there either. She could now turn left and go to the forbidden pond in Farmer Baker's meadow and dip for polliwogs or turn right and go back to the main road that led eventually home. A sound from the left turned her that way. She felt a sun ray caress her arm.

The man was scrawny and wore the kind of clothes Daddies only used when they sawed wood or dug in the garden. The man had a hat pulled down over his eyes so Anna couldn't see what they looked like. He didn't pause when he saw her. Anna stood still watching. The man came up to her. It was the man from the skating rink the man Teddy had said was called Old Man Logan.

"What's in the basket?"

Anna didn't answer.

The man's voice sounded funny, sort of like he was laughing at Anna.

"Those are pretty flowers. Are you going up to the main road?" The road led home.

Anna didn't answer but the man didn't seem to notice.

"Come on. I'll walk you. You shouldn't be alone in the bush."

Anna he had seen him on Main Street. Sometimes he hung around the Convent's yard looking through the fence. The boys from the school across the road made fun of him and dared him to climb the fence.

Anna turned obediently and walked toward the main road. The man sauntered beside her. He smelled stinky-dry and swamp-sweaty all at once.

"What's your name?"

Anna didn't answer.

The man kept talking but Anna didn't listen. She was thinking about Mumma and wondering if she had finished her beads and whether she would be rocking in the green chair or starting to bake another pie. No, she never baked a pie when the day was hot. She would probably go over to Cruickshank's store and buy a jelly-roll for supper.

The man said, "I like your dress. I like blue."

He bent sideways and put his fingers up under her dress and between her legs.

"What do you have here?"

Anna took a deep, sharp breath and stopped dead. The man didn't pause. He kept going. He didn't look back. If he did, Anna would drop the basket and run into the trees where she knew lots of places to hide. But the man didn't stop.

When Anna got home, Mumma was putting knives and forks on the table for supper. She turned. Her soft eyes shadowed.

"How was the picnic?"

"It was all right."

"Where's your basket?"

"I had some flowers in it. They died. I threw them away."

Mumma turned from the table and crossed to sit in the rocking chair. Anna went to stand in front of her.

"Come. I'll give you a rock."

"I'm too big?"

"You're not too big."

Mumma took Anna on her knee. Anna put her hot head against the blue, white-dotted material of Mumma's house-dress. Mumma put her arms around Anna and took her dirty hands in her own cool clean ones.

The green rocking chair rocked. Anna closed her eyes.

Chapter 9

MEAN PEOPLE

Summer 1945

Anna felt angry when Nana told her that, from now on, Aunt Beverly and Emma would be staying permanently at her house. Nana didn't say why and Anna didn't bother her with questions because lately Nana had not been herself. She wanted to be left alone, and she wore her black dress all the time and once Anna had come upon her pulling weeds in the tulip patch, and there were tears trickling down Nana's wrinkled cheeks.

She probably was crying because she would have to put up with Aunt Beverly forever.

This solution for Nana's unhappiness had come to Anna while she was planting her lilac tree. Anna loved lilacs. Their heavenly smell went up her narrow nose, down her throat and clutched at her heart. Nana had lots of lilacs, but there were none in Anna's yard.

Anna had asked Mumma, "If you put a part of a lilac tree in the ground, would it grow?"

Mumma was embroidering the edge of a pillow case and pierced her finger when Anna pounced on her with this question. "Of course it will," she said testily sticking her finger in her mouth.

So Anna broke a branch off one of Nana's trees and planted it beside Mumma's maple. She hauled a dishpan full of water from the creek and dumped it on the branch. That evening the lilacs had wilted into tiny wrinkled, drooping, purple sacs and the leaves had curled up, too. Anna spent the evening dumping water on the lilac branch but the stubborn thing wouldn't grow. She finally plucked it out and threw it into the creek.

"Darned lilac, anyway!"

She plopped herself down and began to sing quietly a song Teddy had taught her.

"Nobody loves me
Everybody hates me
Sitting in the garden eating worms.
Big fat sloppy ones
Little thin juicy ones
Golly how they wiggle when they squirm."

Perhaps it was this mood which brought to mind Aunt Beverly. This pretty woman with silky blonde curls and the body of a grown-up doll had a heart of marble and a tongue that cut like Uncle Patrick's jack-knife. Her words hurt a lot, like the time she told Anna that she had a witch's nose, or the time she led Anna upstairs and showed her a Christmas doll hidden under Mumma's bed when Anna said she believed in Santa Claus. Once when little Emma had been just the teeniest bit naughty, Aunt Beverly said to her, "I hope you die and go to hell!"

Sometimes Aunt Beverly could be as sweet as a mouthful of honey mixed with maple syrup. It made you gag because you suspected she didn't mean it. For this reason, Anna talked back a lot to Aunt Beverly and got away with it. Aunt Beverly was also a liar. Lately she had been going around with a martyred face and pretending she couldn't eat her supper though Anna caught her eating gooseberries dipped in sugar back of Nana's shed.

One day, Anna had been just about to rap on Nana's screened summer-kitchen door when she heard Aunt Beverly whining inside. "I shall not wear this horrible black dress another day. I look ugly, ugly, ugly!"

"It is your behaviour that is ugly, my girl, and I swear by St. Joseph and all the blessed saints, that I will slap you silly if I ever catch you hurting Emma again!"

"I shall have to protect Emma forever, I suppose," Anna said as she plunked herself down under the maple tree.

It had turned into a glorious summer despite Aunt Beverly and Old Man Logan. Anna had now grown big enough to go and visit Charlotte in her pink stucco house near the church and Tess in the dark apartment above the restaurant. Charlotte was sweet and malleable and so was her mother, a tall fair lady with a long face and a big bum who went to work and let Charlotte have friends in while she was away. Their house was always sunny and bright and they had multi-coloured rugs on the floor instead of linoleum. In the living room Anna saw a picture of Charlotte's Daddy who had been killed flying an airplane in the war. Anna wondered how everyone could be so happy if their Daddy was dead. She decided that sometimes you couldn't really tell what people were thinking inside.

Now Tess's mother was totally different. She had long black hair and dusky skin like Mrs. Stuart. Her eyes were smoky dark, and she moved smooth and mysterious like evening mist over the creek behind Anna's house. She didn't smile ever but glided as silent as a shadow around her dark apartment with its clean but shabby furniture. She never offered cookies or sweets, but she always gave Anna a drink of cool water after she climbed the many stairs to the apartment. Anna decided that Tess's mother liked to be private, but she also knew somehow that if she were in trouble, Mrs. Sauvé would rescue her. Tess's brother laughed a lot through glistening white teeth and acted kind in an offhand way. No one ever mentioned a father.

Once Anna asked Tess, "How come you go to the Convent?" not wanting to add *if you're so poor.*

Tess said, "I guess it's because I'm smart and Mother wants me to be a nurse someday. She thinks you get the best education at the Convent."

"You are smart, and I wish I had dark eyes like yours. I guess I'm smart, too, and so is Charlotte. That's why the nuns are letting us skip grade three. Poor Bitsy isn't smart but she's a good friend.

"Can you come walk the track with me today?"

Anna was now suggesting a big sin. When she had been a baby of six years, Mumma used to have quiet fits about kids walking the track that followed the Ottawa River along Main Street, but at one point sent a branch south which crossed the Anishinabe River and Dunkeld Creek before turning east once more and working its way along a ravine that paralleled Maple Street behind Charlie Stuart's and Cousin Bridget's and Nana's houses. Mumma warned her about chuffing engines that hid just around bends and came rushing across trestles to swoop down and cut off tiny feet caught in railroad ties. And Mumma always knew when Anna had walked home by the track, and she would meet Anna at the door, her hands wringing her apron, her eyes afraid and sad, too. It took a long time for Anna to realize that if she wiped soot from her uniform and doubled back behind Charlie Stuart's house, Mumma would just think she had been dawdling and telling herself stories.

But the track was an irresistible place for adventure, with tarry smells and rails to walk and mysterious undergrowth, which could be hiding all sorts of trolls and dragons. Once a train had come along while Anna and Teddy Fisher were walking the trestle across Dunkeld Creek down at the foot of Maple Street.

"Run," Teddy screamed. He started to gallop with the awkward tread necessary to keep to the cross-ties and not jamb a leg through into thin air. Then he turned and saw Anna frozen. He turned back, grabbed her arm, and dragged her along, both of them yelling and crying with boogies running out of their noses. They reached the end of the trestle and leaped sideways into the graveled depression that formed the creek's bank. Anna turned her ankle and ripped her ribbed stockings. She was real mad at Teddy when the engine came chugging slowly up the track like an old black cow going to pasture and the engineer and fireman waved at them with big grins on their faces.

Anna was pulled back to the present by Tess repeating, "My mother wouldn't like me to walk the tracks."

"But once Ruby Flaherty climbed right up into the train when it was stopped and out the other side. And Teddy Fisher says he crawled under the train once."

Tess shrugged. "You go if you want."

"I guess not."

Anyway, it was a happy summer until the army brats moved into Cousin Bridget's house and Colleen and Anna inherited Cousin Bridget's old bicycle. Cousin Bridget herself had met and wed a Métis trapper from Golden Lake by the name of Louis Sauvé. Tess told Anna that Louis was her cousin, and Anna was glad because this would make Tess sort of Anna's cousin, too. Cousin Bridget and Louis were married secretly in Ottawa, even though Louis was a Catholic. Mumma hugged them both when they came to call, but Aunt Beverly said she would never speak to Bridget again, and Nana fed them tea biscuits and walked the floor when they went home. Anna liked Louis. He looked dark and handsome and had a romantic, whispery accent. Anyway, Bridget moved to Pembroke after giving Anna and Colleen her blue bicycle and renting her house to an army wife whose husband was in France saving the French. Her name was Mrs. Jones.

Mrs. Jones never came out of her house, but her yard was overrun by her four boys. Some were Anna's age and some older, and they all looked alike with straw-coloured hair, coined sized freckles, and big shoulders. At first, Anna thought they were okay because they were always putting on Tarzan shows in Cousin Bridget's shed. They would wear their swimming trunks and hang from ropes with knots on them and do a lot of roaring and swinging. They charged one penny entrance fee. Charlie, however, avoided them and they wouldn't play with Teddy who they called a dirty little creep.

One day, Anna and Colleen had a fight about the bicycle. Colleen could ride it and was even allowed to take it off the block to Ruby's house. Annie could not ride and Colleen would not teach her. That day, Anna begged her in her nicest voice to stay and teach her how to ride.

"I will not. This is my bicycle!"

"Is not." This was not just an ordinary fight. This was important. This was unfair.

"Get out of my way."

Ann picked up a stone and threw it at Colleen. It hit her just above her eye. Ruby, who had stood by watching this altercation with great satisfaction, shrieked. Colleen fell off the bicycle, put her hand to her forehead, found the blood, and started to wail. Mumma came running out of the house and Anna raced to hide in the woodshed. She sat there for a very long time, knowing that this time she had gone too far, this time she would be spanked. Over an hour went by before Ruby came softly to the shed door.

"Anna."

Anna climbed out from behind the woodpile. Ruby looked sort of scared.

"I'm coming. Is Colleen killed?"

"No."

Anna swallowed hard and marched to the back door. Colleen waited there inside the door. She, too, looked scared and she had white adhesive tape on her forehead. Anna brushed past her and started up the stairs. The door to Mumma's kitchen door was open and Mumma stood there. Suddenly both Ruby and Colleen began to weep and moan.

"Don't spank her Mrs. Dunkeld!"

"Please, Mumma, don't spank her."

Anna reached the top of the stairs. Mumma took her hand. Then Anna's tears came. "I didn't mean to hurt her, Mumma. But I deserve to be spanked. I made blood!"

Mumma said, "Now the three of you get in here. And I want no more fighting about that bicycle."

"Yes, Mumma"

"Yes, Mumma."

"Yes, Mrs. Dunkeld."

Two days later Teddy Fisher hooked their bicycle and took it for a ride around the village. Colleen and Anna scoured the neighbourhood asking all the kids if they had seen the bicycle. No one had. Charlie helped them look and soon the Jones boys, sensing trouble, came along. They were all in front of Charlie's house when Teddy rode up the hill as bold as a dog with a stolen bone.

"There's the dirty little creep!" yelled a Jones Boy.

"Let's get him," cried another.

"Filthy little thief!"

"Better run."

But Teddy didn't run. He climbed down off the bicycle as they encircled him. They began pushing and shoving him, rubbing dirt on his face. He stood there his hazel eyes as cold as winter.

Charlie cried, "Hey that's enough."

"Want some, too, Sissy?"

One of the Jones boys ran into Cousin Bridget's shed and came out carrying a jar full of wasps captured for their next Tarzan show.

"Get him down. Hold him!"

"No" shrieked Anna. They were shaking the wasps down the back of Teddy's shirt. She went for them, yelling and striking out with her fists, her shoes, trying to yank at their short straw hair, to tear them away from Teddy. "It's not your bike! Stop it!"

Shocked, the Jones boys let go of their victim and Teddy tore the shirt off. There were red welts on his back. Wasps darted every which way. Kids ran in all directions, squealing.

Anna ended sobbing on Mumma's lap. "Why did they do that, Mumma. Why?"

Mumma said nothing just held her close and began humming, *"Toura loura loura. Toura loura li. Toura loura loura. It's an Irish lullaby ..."*

A few days later Teddy and his mother moved out of the house up the street. Some said Teddy's daddy had come home. Others said his mother had taken up with a soldier.

Chapter 10

THE BLUE HAT

Autumn 1945

Anna was playing in the cloakroom. It was small, and there was a window, and she liked to play there because she could pretend it was her house. Once when she was little she pretended she was St. Bernadette and made a cave with chairs and a sheet in the cloakroom. She lit a candle and closed her eyes really tight and imagined she saw the Blessed Virgin. The candle set fire to the sheet.

Mumma scared her. She yanked her out of there and stomped on the fire and got a pot of water and threw it on it. And she yelled at Anna. Anna was surprised. Colleen yelled at her, but Mumma never yelled and never got mad. Her hands were soft and warm, and her voice was like her heartbeat, slow and quiet and safe.

Anna didn't stay scared long, but she guessed Mumma thought she was because she picked her up, even if she was getting pretty heavy, and carried her to the green rocking-chair. Mumma rocked Anna for a long time. At first, her heartbeat sounded fast and loud, but it slowed down after a while. Anna thought she was crying, and it made her feel bad. After that, Anna was careful so she wouldn't make Mumma feel bad.

But that was when Anna was small. Today, Mumma was sitting on the front veranda step because of the dreadfully hot weather. She had her stockings rolled down, and sometimes she pulled out the front of her blue dress with the bumpy white polka dots and blew down it. Mumma only did this if no one but Anna was looking. She didn't mind Anna seeing.

Before she left the cloakroom, Anna looked up to the shelf to make sure her hat was there. It was a special hat, blue, with a beautiful greenish duck feather stuck under the band, just like Uncle Patrick's hat. But best of all, it was shaped like a boat, just like the hat her Daddy wore in the picture.

Anna left the cloakroom and went into the living room. She didn't like the living room much because it had a picky brown couch and a chair that always smelled dusty. And an ugly lamp. But it also had the upright piano that had once belonged to Nana's mother, and the pictures. Anna made sure that Mumma wasn't coming in, and then she climbed on the piano-stool. Mumma didn't like Anna to climb there because she said that she'd fall. Anna never fell, but Mumma always thought she would.

She looked at the family picture first.

There was Daddy with his arm around Mumma. She had on the pretty black velvet dress with the embroidered flowers on the neck. Daddy had on his blue uniform and his blue hat. Anna didn't like this picture. Mumma and Daddy looked sad. Anna looked happy though. She was sort of small, and had fat legs and short tight curls. Anna remembered that when she was real little, big people always used to ask here where she got her curls, and she would tell them that her hair was *naturally* curly, and they laughed at her. They laughed at her when she said *embroidered,* too. It was hard to understand big people sometimes.

Anyway, in the picture, she had on a knitted dress. It was black in the picture, but Mumma had told her that it was really red. She sort of remembered it, but it was gone now.

Anna thought, I hate the way clothes are always gone when you get bigger. I want a new red, knitted dress. Maybe sometime I'll ask Mumma for one.

In the picture, Colleen had on her brown velvet dress. When the picture was taken, before Daddy went away, Colleen went to school and Anna didn't, but Anna went to the Convent sometimes with Mumma to pay the bill. Anna liked going there. An old nun with a kind face answered the door. Anna later learned she was Sister Mary Dorothy. She knew Anna's name. She knew Mumma's, too, because Mumma went to school at the Convent when she was a little girl. Nana Jeanne went there, too, in the olden days. The old nun always took them into a parlour with rich furniture and lots of green ferns on stands. It smelled good, like wax. Best of all, there was a big picture all the way to the ceiling. It was the first thing you saw when you came in the front door. It was sad but really nice and dark.

Anna asked Mumma, and she said, "It's Jesus on the Cross."

"Who's Jesus?"

Mumma said, "*Jesus is God*" like he was really special.

Anna asked Mumma. "Is Jesus magic like Santa Claus?"

"He is better than magic. The Spirit of Christmas is magic, but Jesus is God. Bad people put Jesus on the cross, and he let them so everyone can go to heaven when they die."

"I guess the bad people were Germans."

Germans were the people who started the war that Anna's Daddy and Uncle Matthew were gone away to. Anna liked her Uncle Matthew a lot. He always acted jolly and laughed and told stories. His breath smelt like plum preserves and peppermint. He used to give her a whole nickel sometimes. He used to be mean to Aunt Beverly sometimes, but you couldn't help being mean to Aunt Beverly. Now Uncle Matthew was gone to war, too. He had a brown hat just like her Daddy's blue hat.

Anna was a big girl now. She was skipping grade three. But before she got to go to school at the Convent, Anna had sent Daddy a piece of her *naturally* curly hair in a letter. She could sort of print, but she couldn't read yet. Mumma printed on a paper and Anna copied it on another paper. Daddy gave her hair to a plane pilot so he could put it in his pocket when he flew over the Germans to drop a bomb on them.

Maybe it was Charlotte's daddy. Anna wondered if it hurt the Germans when he dropped bombs on them.

Anna thought, I better hurry because Mumma will come in soon, and she'll look sad if she catches me on the piano-stool.

Anna looked at the other picture, the one she liked. It was Daddy. He was smiling. And he had on the blue hat, but it was grey in the picture. Colleen said that he was brave, and he could get killed in the war, and then he wouldn't come home. Anna thought what it would be like if Daddy got killed. Would she cry? She squeezed her eyes closed and tried to make tears come. She tried to feel really sad. She made her eyes a little wet.

Colleen must be lying, even if it's a sin. Daddy will never get killed like Charlotte's daddy. If Hubert Dumice or a German hits Daddy, Daddy will sock him right in the nose.

Anna went to the door to see if Mumma was coming in. She could only see her back. She was looking at a big boy on a new bicycle. Not many people had bicycles unless they got an old one from their Cousin Bridget. But it was fair that the big boy had a new bicycle because he delivered telegrams. Big people said he was slow, and that's why he didn't go to the war. Anna thought he must have tricked them because he could sure go fast on that bicycle.

Mumma stood up. The boy brought a paper to her. She didn't even say Thank you, and Anna was sort of ashamed for her. Mumma always made *her* say Thank you.

Anna opened the screen door and gave the big boy her best smile because Mumma didn't thank him. His mouth smiled back but his eyes didn't.

He said, "Do you want me to get someone, Missus?"

Mumma shook her head and he went away.

"What is it Mumma? What's the paper?"

But Mumma didn't answer. Instead she grabbed Anna's arm and jerked her down the steps and started running down the path.

Anna yelled, "Mumma, you're hurting me!"

Mumma stopped and looked at Anna. Her face was really white and ugly. Anna started to cry. Anybody would cry if her Mumma looked like that.

Then Mumma's face was pretty again, but still white. She said, "Can you run, Anna?"

"Pretty fast." But Anna was scared it wouldn't be fast enough.

Mumma walked quickly down the street under the maples. She was holding Anna's hand really tight. There were nice red and yellow leaves on the sidewalk. Anna wanted to pick them up. She saw her mother's face. She was crying.

"Don't cry, Mumma. I didn't do anything bad."

"It's not you, Anna."

Anna didn't say anything else.

When they got to Nana's house, Mumma made Anna sit on the veranda step when she went in. Anna sneaked up and listened at the screen door.

Nana cried out, "No, not Richard, too!"

"No, Mother. No. He has a head wound."

Nana's voice shook when she said, "He'll be all right."

Mumma said, "But a head injury."

Then Anna couldn't hear anything else because Nana came out and sent her to pick mums in her garden. She said Anna could pick all the flowers she wanted. Anna should have been happy, but she wasn't.

Anna didn't want to ask Mumma any more questions, so she asked Colleen who said, "Don't be so stupid. "Somebody dropped a bomb on him in England."

"On his head?"

"Of course not! If it fell on his head, he'd be dead like ... but he could die anyway, so don't you bother Mumma with questions!"

Anna went and sat in the cloakroom on the floor under the coats. *Daddies don't die!* But she knew that they did.

She had to ask *someone* so she asked Colleen again. "I told you."

"Yes, but our Daddy won't die." Anna started to weep.

Colleen didn't call her *bawl-baby* like usual. She looked like she wanted to tell Anna something and then told her something else. "You know Charlotte Green's Daddy died in the war already."

Anna dragged a chair into the cloakroom and got down her blue hat. Mumma asked why she was wearing her hat in the house.

"I want my Daddy to see it when he comes home."

"You just keep wearing it, Anna."

When winter came and there was lots of snow, Mumma took Anna and her big sister to Nana's house. They got to sleep there! Aunt Beverly had taken Emma and gone home to Ottawa to visit her cousin, so Anna got to sleep in her Uncle Matthew's old bed. Anna liked his bed because it had a slippery red cover on it that shone like jelly. And all his good stuff was there. There were soldier pictures, and big boy toys, and pictures of Anna and Emma on the dresser. Funny though, his brown hat was there, too, on the dresser. There was a velvet covered box beside it. Anna opened the box. She saw a big coin-like thing hanging on a striped ribbon.

Anna asked Nana, "Why is Uncle Matthew's brown hat here?"

Nana's face got really hard like a statue, but not beautiful like the Blessed Virgin's statue.

"He doesn't need it now."

Anna didn't ask any more questions.

In the middle of the night, Colleen woke her up and told her to number one in the toilet, then Nana helped her dress. Her hands weren't soft and gentle like Mumma's, but Anna didn't mind. They went outside in the dark! Uncle Patrick put them in Uncle Matthew's car and they drove away. Anna snuggled against Colleen because there were white clouds in front of their faces, even in the car. They went to the train station. Uncle Patrick carried Anna to the edge of the platform near the track and then put her down. Anna coughed because the cold got in her mouth. Nana held her hand, and Colleen held her other hand. Anna wanted to go to sleep.

She got scared when the train came because it rumbled the ground, and it was big and black and screechy, not like the old black cow trains on the branch track near Maple Street. Then a man put a stool in front of the door, and opened the door, and out came Mumma, right out of the train! Anna couldn't see very well because there were so many legs. But Mumma came and big gloves reached down and picked Anna up, and she could see over all the heads.

He's awful big!

He's got on a blue hat!

Chapter 11

RICHARD

1959

The summer of 1959 is a time to tear your heart out. Colleen is troubled and trying to hide it, which makes it all the more pitiful. Instead of starting a newer and happier life now that the divorce from her monster of a husband has come through and she has found safe shelter in Dunkeld House, she wanders numb through the life they all share. Aroused only by her twins, she devotes herself slavishly to them and, in Anna's opinion, spoils them.

But didn't Mumma spoil us? Anna's Inner Voice asks. Or can you call it spoiling when a child knows nothing but gentleness and love? Did it make you weak so that you were ambushed by life's realities or did it make you strong so that, no matter what happened, you found an inherent power in the knowledge that goodness, no matter how rare, does exist? But where is the reward for goodness? Mumma lies uncomplaining, her lungs slowly rotting away, her heart getting larger and larger until it threatens to burst from her chest. Colleen is a refugee from one of life's sickening realities, marital abuse. Thank god that bugger never touched the twins, at least not with his fists, just with his whip of a tongue.

And my little Rachel is as alienated from me as if I had never given birth to her. Always a little stranger, even at my breast. So meticulous and serious like a tiny old woman. So lost. Does she miss the only father she ever knew? She sees him often enough. Maybe she would be better with him.

No. I can't do that.

Bridget and Louis. Why can't they live in peace? God punish those who hate native people just because they are natives. Can they not see the strength that is Louis? Can they not see Tess struggling through medical school with none to help but her hard working brother who does what he can? But they do not see. And God does not punish them. At least Bridget and Louis are happy here and what would we do without Bridget to supervise Mumma's care? And Beverly's! She wandered all the way to the edge of town last week before Charlotte passed her on the road and brought her safe home in her car. But one couldn't stick Beverly into some institution. They would just have to lock their own front gate no matter how inconvenient it proved.

And my Emma? Where did this savage rebellion come from? She doesn't yell or scream or rant against her family as many youngsters are starting to do. She simply goes her own way quietly and almost with grace. But the drinking and even perhaps, surely not, drugs?

Anna looks at the picture of her father on Nana's piano, so young, so handsome in his Airforce uniform. If only you were here, Daddy, or some man, any man to save me? Anna laughs. Such as sentiment. Coming from me?

1946

Richard and Annie were down in Mrs. Dumice's cellar pulling the curly white sprouts off the eyes of some potatoes.

"These are for the Precious Blood Nuns, eh Daddy?" Richard nodded. "How come we have to give them our potatoes?"

"Well they rang the bell at their little convent, and that means they are short of food and all Catholics should bring them what they can."

"The priests have lots of food. How come they let the nuns get hungry?"

"Well, it's not that simple. You see, these nuns take a vow of poverty which means they allow themselves only the bare necessities of life, and they are not allowed to ask for help until they are starving."

"Nana says they aren't even allowed to talk."

"Yes."

"I don't think I'll be a Precious Blood nun when I grow up. Why do they act that way?"

"Well, they believe that by devoting their lives to prayer, they can make up for our sins."

"Doesn't seem fair to me."

"I don't think you'll ever have to worry about giving up talking, Anna."

Later Daddy went out to split wood and put it in the shed. Anna tagged along. She never wanted to be far away from this fascinating person who was so big and strong and who knew everything about everything. "Can I help, Daddy?"

"This is sort of hard work for a little girl."

"I'm really strong. I can do it."

"Go and ask your mother for some gardening gloves so you won't get slivers in your fingers."

Daddy let her ride to the Precious Blood Convent in Uncle Patrick's car when he delivered the potatoes, and he took her to the village ice house where blocks of ice wrapped in burlap were piled to the ceiling, and the smell of damp and sawdust made a different shadowy world. Anna wanted to experience all the worlds there were and Daddy seemed to understand this. When Daddy and Mumma went for walks, Daddy would carry Anna on his shoulders even though Mumma said she was too heavy.

Anna would shout, "I can touch the sky!"

And when the older kids took Anna and Colleen on the *Oiseau* ferry to Érable Island on the Ottawa River, Daddy didn't warn them to be careful or anything. He just said, "You are big girls, so use your common sense." And they did, learning where the poison ivy was situated near the wonderful wide sandy beaches and putting their bottles of pop in the water to keep them cool and never missing the ferry home.

Anna felt safe.

Once she came into the kitchen and saw Mumma sitting on Daddy's knee. They both smiled at her sort of funny. Anna sort of liked it but couldn't figure out why. Was Daddy just giving Mumma a rock?

"Mrs. Flaherty says we can have their cottage on Érable for a week if we take Ruby with us," Mumma said.

They were eating supper in the big green kitchen. Mumma painted it every second summer and she always painted it green. Supper was boiled chicken and dumplings and apple pie and Queen Anne cake. Mumma made big suppers now that Daddy had come home, and he had to have extra pie and stuff for his lunch pail when he went to work at the Atomic Energy Plant at Chalk River.

"The girls will love that. But how about you?"

Mumma's face got all prissy like it did when she was nervous. "There aren't many cottages on that part of the island."

"Will you mind being alone?"

"No, of course not."

But she did mind. Anna was in ecstasy, living in a world of sun and hot, brown-sugary sand, and hammocks among the pines, and raccoons, and ducks in the bay, and turtles you could stand on in the river just like they were rocks. Colleen and Ruby spent all their time sitting on logs gabbing about boys and reading comics. But Anna didn't mind being by herself. She wandered and dug sand and told herself a million stories about pirates and fairies who lived in sandcastles. She even wrote a secret message to Bitsy on a piece of birchbark, put it in a bottle and threw it into the river. Surely some lumberman would find it and deliver it to Bitsy in Dunkeld Village.

At night, Mumma listened to the battery radio and had every coal oil lamp in the cottage lit. She even said her beads while the girls did picture puzzles, played Snakes and Ladders, Monopoly, and Old Maid.

Anna asked Colleen," Is Mumma scared of something?"

"Anna, don't bother Mumma."

Anna went out on the screened-in porch. A big moon spread light all over the river in wiggly lines, and the air was clean-damp and piney. It made your nose feel clear. She got a flashlight and walked down to the outhouse. It felt sort of nice spooky in there with the light bouncing back from the walls and the spiders running for cover. On her way back she heard a clunky sound on the river and stopped. There was a shadow like a boat and a black figure in it. Someone was rowing. She trotted to the cottage.

"Daddy's coming. Daddy's coming."

"Don't be silly, Anna."

But it was Daddy. He dragged the boat up on the sand and came sauntering up the path. "Just thought you might like some company for the weekend."

Mumma leaped off the porch and right into Daddy's arms. Colleen and Ruby giggled but Anna didn't. She thought Daddy very brave.

"You didn't row all the way from Dunkeld?" Mumma asked when she had stopped hugging Daddy.

"A good night for a river trip."

The next day Daddy took Anna out in the boat to do some fishing off the point. Anna wore a big hat with a straw daisy on top to shield her from the sun. At first Daddy tried to teach her to put a worm on the hook, but Anna said that she didn't like to see the worm suffer so Daddy got a silver thing from his fishing box and put it on instead.

"How come we're Catholics even if we have a Scottish name?"

Daddy looked at her as much as to say, *Where do you get all these* questions? But he didn't say that. "You think we should be Presbyterian? I can understand that. You see, when Great Grampa Dunkeld came from Scotland, he was all alone and he married an Irish girl for company. When she was dying, he became a Catholic to please her."

"Was that Poor Sean?"

Daddy's lips got smiley. "No. It was his father, Angus."

Anna opened her mouth to ask another question but shut it. If she were quiet she had learned, Daddy would tell a really good story. And so he did.

"In 1858 Angus Dunkeld came to Canada to seek his fortune on a big sailing ship. Times were hard in Scotland and being the youngest son, he had to be the one to leave. He landed at Quebec and took steamers up the Ottawa to Pembroke and then a canoe up to Dunkeld Village, which was a wilderness then. At first he worked like a slave in the lumber camps and then he married and started a farm where Dunkeld House stands today."

"What's Dunkeld House?"

"I'll take you to look at it some day."

"Your Great Grandfather was a clever and hardworking man and by the end of his life he owned three farms, a hotel, and a livery stable and had established Dunkeld Village. His son's used to draw supplies to the lumber camps from his farms."

"I guess he was rich, eh Daddy?"

"Rich according to our lights now."

"What happened?"

"Well the railroad came through and the lumber camps moved further west and there was a depression and in the end, Angus had to break up his holdings among his sons. They couldn't make a go of it, so my father, Sean, your Grampa, left to work in the mills in Sudbury. He died there of the flu leaving Mother penniless and with three boys to raise."

"That was you and Uncle Patrick and Uncle Matthew?"

A pause. "Yes."

"Where is Uncle Matthew, Daddy?"

Daddy put his hand under the big hat with the daisy and lifted Anna's chin until he could see into her eyes. "I think you know, Anna."

"He got killed in the war?"

"Yes."

"And that's why Nana is so sad?"

"Yes. That's why."

"And now we're stuck with Aunt Beverly."

"Just a minute, now, young lady. Your Aunt has special problems of her own and she can't really help the way she is. You must try to be good to her."

"But why? Because the Catechism says so?"

"It has nothing to do with religion. It is simply how decent people behave, how a Dunkeld would behave."

Strangely enough, this made Anna feel all special and shiny inside.

It seemed her world was blessed.

That year winter laid a severe hand on Dunkeld Village but in mid-January there was a thaw and Anna tried out her new bobsled on the Precious Blood Nuns' hill, which leaned towards the Anishinabe River. Of course it was strictly forbidden to go out on the ice, so every day after school, Anna coaxed Bitsy down the hillside under the Maple Street Bridge, and they climbed and slid their way among the heaved ice floes on the Anishinabe River and crawled breathing like race horses up the other side.

"You're going to get killed, Anna!" Colleen scolded.

"The ice is thick. I'm not stupid."

"I'll tell Daddy." But Anna knew she wouldn't. Daddy was far too important a person to be bothered with such kid stuff. And, of course, you didn't tell Mumma anything because she would get all worried and fret.

One night Ruby and Anna went skating at the arena without Colleen who had an earache. Mumma put warm electric oil in Colleen's ear and a piece of cotton batting. Anna had inherited Cousin Bridget's old tube skates and she could careen around the rink with the best, always taking the dangerous place at the end of the whip in Crack the Whip. She would skate with Charlie, holding his wet mittened hand but she hated all the other boys.

That night Charlie wasn't there and Annie saw Old Man Logan sitting in the stands smoking cigarettes. She had never told anyone about that day in Baker's Bush. She couldn't imagine what words to use with a grownup and kids wouldn't believe her or even worse they *would* believe her. But when she and Ruby left the arena after skating, Old Man Logan was standing on the other side of the road watching.

"Walk on this side."

"Why?" asked Ruby.

"Because there's a bad man over there."

Ruby believed Anna immediately. Kids knew when you were serious. "I'm scared," she whispered.

"Never mind. We shall stay on this side of the street." They began walking up the ice-rutted hill toward home. Old Man Logan kept pace with them, watching like a weasel stalking chickens. They could see him grin when he stopped under a street light. When they paused, he paused. When they ran, he quickened his steps.

"Don't show you're scared."

"But we have to cross over when we get to your house, and I have to walk all the rest of the way home alone," Ruby whimpered.

"We'll pretend to go into Charlie's house and he'll go away."

They did this, hiding behind Charlie's hedge. After a long time, Anna peeked out. "He's gone."

"But I'm scared to go home alone."

"Well come on then." They ran across the street, up the path, up the porch steps, and in through Anna's front door. They went right to Daddy who was reading the newspaper in the living room.

"Daddy, there's a bad man outside."

Daddy leaped to his feet. He didn't even put on a coat or galoshes. He ran out the front door.

However, he came back after a little time and said, "I don't see anyone out there. You girls must be imagining things."

What do you say to an adult when they don't believe you? Ruby went outside. Three minutes later she came squealing back. "He's up around the corner."

Anna could tell Daddy still didn't believe her, but he put on his coat and his big gum rubbers and walked home with Ruby.

That night Anna had her first nightmare. In it, a black figure chased her, but just when long-fingered hands were reaching out to get her, she flapped her arms, leaped into the air, and flew off like the Angel Gabriel himself.

In February, news came by telephone from Érable Island that one of the few farmers left there had been burned out and the family was destitute. The other islanders were doing what they could, but a child was awful sick and they needed help. Father Duke, Daddy, and another man from the church collected food and clothing and medicine, hitched two horses to a sleigh and made for the island in the darkness. The ice didn't hold. The horses, the sleigh, and the men in it went through into the merciless river. They found the bodies snagged in a bay just west of Deep River in the spring.

Chapter 12

THE BROACH

1947

Faith's grief after Richard's death made her distant but she remained as kindly as ever. She was smoking again like she did during the war. The thumb and first two fingers on her right hand were stained dirty yellow. She rolled her own cigarettes in a contraption made of wood and rubber, cutting them with Richard's unused razor blades. Sometimes Anna helped her, trying to get close.

"I smoked once with Charlie," she confessed. "We made cigarettes out of oak leaves."

"Oh, Anna. All children do that. I did it myself." This was not what Anna wanted to hear.

Anna was growing up. She was ten years old and got an allowance of a quarter. A returning veteran had gotten permission to set up a screen in the Town Hall every Saturday and show movies. Anna went to the Saturday afternoon matinee movie with Bitsy and bought a bag of popcorn and a lemon-lime pop. It was usually a double feature, and they sometimes stayed through two showings until seven o'clock … until Bitsy got a licking for it. Anna was in love with Roy Rogers and also with a boy at the Separate School who, she thought, looked like Roy Rogers. The boy returned this love by throwing wads of chewed gum at her during the movie. She saw Teddy Fisher once during a Hopalong Cassidy movie. He stuck his thumbs in his ears and wiggled his fingers at her. She had to bite her lips not to smile. Charlie Stuart wasn't allowed to go to movies and was always off on ventures such as soapbox derbies and decorate your bicycle parades. Anna worried that Charlie was becoming a drip.

But Mumma remained distant, Nana had no time for Anna, and Colleen wouldn't be caught dead with her. Anna started to spend more and more time lying around on her bed, eating Crispy Crunch chocolate bars, five-cent bags of potato chips and drinking Pure Spring Gingerale. Food got very important suddenly. She and Bitsy would sometimes go without popcorn at the movies and drop into Joe Ching's restaurant on Main Street. This was the local hangout for the teenagers from the Convent and the Boy's School and the Collegiate, that is, for those who lived in the east part of the village where the lumber baron mansion was. Anna's house was in the humbler part of the east-end on the very edge of the village. The kids from the west side of the Anishinabe River met in the Astrolabe Café. They were mostly boys with poor haircuts and girls whose fathers were Métis or Italian or French. German and Dutch kids didn't go to restaurants. Tess's mother worked in the Astrolabe Café. This was another reason for not going there. One couldn't be waited upon by one's friend's mother.

The in-crowd to which Colleen and Ruby belonged sat at round tables at the front of the restaurant, boys on one side, girls on the other. Everyone smoked forbidden cigarettes and ordered French-fries and Coke. The smart aleck boys often stuffed their bills down behind the radiators and didn't pay.

Anna and Bitsy sat at the back in the booths with sticky green seats. These were for strangers and little kids. Anna always ordered a Tin Roof which was three rounded mounds of vanilla ice cream, one coated with marshmallow sauce, one with butterscotch, and one with chocolate. Crushed nuts were sprinkled over this and a cherry stuck on the centre mound, which was always butterscotch. This was served with big glasses of iced water. It cost the remainder of Anna's allowance but it was worth it. Once the movie was a Walt Disney and Anna took Emma along and laughed when Emma's eyes rounded at seeing her first Tin Roof.

Some Saturdays, they would skip the movie and go to the chip wagon where a guy dumped sliced potatoes in deep sizzling vats of fat and scooped them out in a wire basket. He would throw them on a warming plate and from there into brown paper cones of three sizes, nickel, dime, and quarter. He always doused them with vinegar and salt just before he handed them hot to you, little rounds of grease already seeping through the paper cones. He stuck a toothpick in a top chip for dainty eating.

Sinking your teeth into one of these chips was better than being kissed by Roy Rogers.

Anna looked at herself in the oval mirror with the carved leaves on the rim. "I look fat. I'll soon look like Charlie." This was a fallacy because Charlie had lost his baby plumpness and was going through a growth spurt.

Faith called up the stairs, "Anna, it's a sunny day. You should go out and play."

"Don't want to." The face in the mirror looked very sad indeed. Anna saw tears gather in her eyes. "My Daddy's dead," she said, knowing it would make the tears flow. Who wouldn't cry? The anger boiled and bubbled in her chest until Anna could scarcely breathe. Why did you do it? You stupid. Stupid! Always preaching to me not to go on the ice and then you … It's all your fault! She turned and threw herself on the bed, hiding her hot face in the pillow. She spent the rest of the day lying around reading *Invisible Scarlet O'Neil.* Wouldn't it be great if you could just press a nerve in your wrist and be invisible like Scarlet? School was okay except that Anna got sent to the principal for having food spots on her uniform, and when she offered up a decade of the rosary for a kid who had to go to the dentist, Sister St. Stephen changed it to the repose of the souls in Purgatory.

Was Daddy in Purgatory, burning for all the venial sins he hadn't had time to confess? Criminy Custard, Anna just didn't believe it, and she stood up during Catechism class and told everybody that she didn't believe that babies who weren't baptized went to limbo, a place where they floated around and never got to see God. Sister St. Stephen, a timid soul with red eyebrows, didn't punish Anna for this. Anna also had begun to hate music lessons, so she skipped them. One day in the winter when she went to get her coat in the cloakroom, it was gone. A girl from baby class came and said that Sister Margaret Mary wanted to see Anna.

When she went, Sister Margaret Mary had her coat. "It has come to my attention that you have been missing both practice and lessons, Anna. Why is this?" Sister Margaret Mary was old and skinny and strict and Anna respected her.

What could one say? I hate it? I don't have any talent. No. "I don't know, Sister."

"Well, don't let it happen again."

Why don't you give me the strap? I hate everything!

One day, Bitsy and Anna were walking home from the movies when they passed the old arena. A group of boys from Joe Ching's most select table were sitting against the wall smoking cigarettes. These were the smart-alecky boys whose fathers were doctors or dentists or owned businesses on Main Street, the new rich. They were Colleen's age. Anna secretly thought them desirable and unobtainable.

A boy called, "Hey, Cookie!"

And shame of shames, Anna turned her head.

"Not you dog biscuit." The boys giggled and punched each other. A cold emptiness settled in Anna's chest. From that moment she was convinced that she was ugly.

One day she was getting raisin oatmeal cookies from the kitchen tin when she saw Mumma sitting under the maple. Mumma was bent over like she had been beaten, and her body was shaking. Anna dropped the cookies and raced down the stairs and out to the back stoop. She hesitated. Mumma was sobbing. She crept over to the tree and put her hand on Mumma's head. The dark hair had white strings in it, even though Mumma was still young.

"Mumma, don't cry."

But Mumma couldn't stop. She was sputtering and gasping. She choked out, "What will we do, Anna? What will we do now?"

"Do. We'll just do our best, Mumma."

Mumma got control of herself. "I'm sorry, Anna. Sometimes it is hard to be brave, but I'm all right now. Don't you worry."

That day something cold and hard melted inside Anna. But it was Nana Jeanne who showed her how decent people acted. She took Anna out to Baker's Bush to pick pussy willows, and when they got back to Nana's house, she led Anna upstairs to her room over the kitchen, usually forbidden territory.

She went to the dresser and opened a big black box. She took out something wrapped in black velvet and showed it to Anna. It was a beautiful old amethyst and silver broach.

"This broach belonged to the Dunkeld women. Your grandfather gave it to me to pass on. It came all the way from Scotland. You will give it to another when the time comes and with it you must pass on everything you know about the family."

When Anna showed the broach to Mumma, she hugged her very hard and said, "It won't be easy, Anna, being the strong one, like your Daddy. But I know you can do it."

Anna wanted to ask, "Why do I have to do it?"

1960

Beverly is sitting on a high-backed chair, looking out her bedroom window. In a corner, the small black and white television chatters away like a little alien. Anna crosses to turn it off. Beverly doesn't notice. Anna approaches and kneels by Beverly's side, placing her hand gently on her forearm. One must be careful lest a startled Beverly strike out. Beverly's head turns. Only bewilderment in her eyes. She looks frightened.

"Aunt Beverly, it's me, Anna. Your niece Anna."

A sudden beatific smile. Recognition. "Anna. I'm so glad you came. You have to get me out of here. They keep me locked up, you know. And you haven't come in so very long, you little bugger."

"Aunt Beverly. You know that's not true. I come every day, and I usually bring you up your supper. Don't you remember?"

"Yes. The food's good here. Did you bring me some chocolate?"

Anna pulls the Cadbury Caramilk bar from her apron pocket. "Do I ever forget?"

"I can always count on you." They go through the ritual of taking the paper off the chocolate bar, spreading the silver inner lining on Beverly's lap, and breaking the bar into its little squares, smooth liquid caramel leaking onto the paper. The smell of the chocolate glides delicious into Anna's nostrils.

Beverly offers a piece to Anna. "I can't," Anna says. "I'm on a diet." She always says this. Beverly smiles. For a moment the fear leaves her still china blue eyes, but only for a moment.

"There's something, something, a thing, a, a, a, form?" cupping her hands together. "Oh dear, I have to tell you. Words. Words. A shape."

Anna keeps her voice soft. "Something is bothering you?"

"Yes, that's it." Looks around the room for inspiration. "It's like that," pointing at her narrow bed with the daisy-patterned quilt Emma stitched for her. "I don't know the words."

"Do you have pain?"

"No.

"Now I've got it. It's the man. You know that man?"

Having heard this tale many times, Anna prompts. "You mean your husband, Matthew."

"Do I?"

"Yes, I think so."

A deep breath. "Well that man used to drink whisky, lots of whisky."

"I know."

Frustrated. "No you don't. That isn't it."

Anna sighs. She must listen to the tale again because for Beverly, each time is the first. "Was he mean to you?" She is beginning to feel stifled in the attractive, airy room.

"Yes. That's it. He drank up the food money and I had no milk for … did I have a baby?"

"Yes. Emma. Do you want me to go and get her?"

"No. I can't take care of a baby."

A silence in which Beverly eats the last two chocolate squares. She rubs the caramel off the paper and licks her fingers one by one. She now has the sunny countenance of a contented child. However, clouds scud in. "That man. He would make me lie on the bed and he did things to me. I didn't like it." There are tears in the lovely eyes.

"That's all right, Aunt Beverly. He's dead now. Killed in the war."

"Is there a war?"

Too difficult to explain. "Yes."

"I'm glad."

"I have to go now."

"No."

"I'll come up again with your lunch. Here I'll turn on your television."

"You're a good girl, Anna."

Why the sudden joy in her heart and the feeling of love streaming warm light from her chest? Like pictures of the Blessed Virgin. Because Beverly whom she had always disliked remembered her name? Anna turns on the television and walks toward the door. Already Beverly has forgotten her and is staring out the window.

Emma has been listening in the hall. She is weeping. Anna puts her arms around her.

"Dear Heart, don't carry on so. She's not unhappy really. Anything bad she dreams up is gone in a moment."

Emma shoves her away. "You don't understand. Nobody understands! I'm not sorry for her! I'm glad, glad. Let her suffer. Jesus Christ, let her suffer. She made my life a living hell. I hope she rots. Ogod. Ogod."

Emma had come in drunk the night before, stumbling on the stairs, puking, peeing, and giggling in the bathroom. Anna had gone to her, knocked but heard only, "Leave me the hell alone!" Could this be little Emma, so gentle, so lost in a world of dreams, never complaining, making fantasy her life, her shelter between bouts of ugliness? Better to respect her grief, for grief it was, sorrow for what might have been.

Anna turns away from the bathroom door in time to see Rachel's door quietly closing. And that one? My beloved child. Rachel doesn't break the rules. Rachel is the six-year-old calendar girl for all the rules that ever there were, a model pupil in Grade One at Our Lady of Snows. One must be absolutely clean at all times, in thought, in word, in deed. One must tolerate a weird mother who never goes to church, or hardly ever, and then only when she needs a dose of ritual. One must visit with a dying grandmother, though every moment in her presence made one want to run screaming into the landscape. Live in a house with a great aunt married to a *nigger*, a word learned from her father, another great aunt as nuts as they come. Adoring a father who thinks that the righteous all dwell inside the door of the Presbyterian church, who had tried to save her priest-ridden, statue adoring mother only to have her spit in his face and take his adored girl away from him.

His girl?

But there is nothing to be done for Rachel except to love her. Perhaps when she is older …

"Emma, I want you to come with me." She leads the unprotesting girl down the hall and up the stairs to the top floor. She hauls out her old dolls' suitcase. Before opening it, she tells Emma the story of how she ran away but wasn't allowed to cross the street. Emma smiles and hiccoughs. Opening the case, Anna takes out a black velvet box and opens it. Inside is a very old silver broach, large, tarnished, missing a couple of tiny stones but precious. A large amethyst in the center of a silver flower, looking for all the world like a trillium.

"This belonged to your Great, Great, Grandmother. I want you to have it."

Chapter 13

GROWING UP

1949

Anna is twelve years old. And she has breasts. Beautiful breasts, though she does not realize it. They are becoming the kind of breasts that men yearn after, large above a small waist, full and smooth and cool, heavy but silky, with small pink nipples that need coaxing to rise.

She has her first bra, cotton and white, much bigger than Colleen's who is fifteen years old. Anna knows that Colleen resents this and in some instinctive way knows why. Anna has also had her first period. Mumma made a big fuss about it saying she was a woman now and putting her to bed with a hot water bottle. There was a little bit of cramping but nothing worse than when you ate too much. Anna wondered why some of the older girls at the Convent got very white and had to go home when they got their period. They called it the Curse and talked about agony. There wasn't anything to it really.

Nana Jeanne said, "You are going to be fine figure of a woman, Anna." This was before Anna got fat and decided she was not only ugly, she was repulsive, too.

Boys started to ask her where she got her lumpy sweaters and other stupid stuff. They were drippy boys so there was no thrill in it. The desirable boys ignored her. She hadn't had a crush even from afar on some cute boy from the Protestant High School, for some time. So Anna's body was ready but her imagination lagged uncharacteristically behind.

Strangely enough it was Bitsy who set her on the road to mortal sin and certain damnation. They were sitting on a log at Sandy Point on Érable Island. The other kids were splashing around in the shallow water, the girls squealing and acting the fool. Some kids from the Protestant school were nearby, not mixing but doing a lot of glancing back and forth. Anna saw Teddy diving like a pink streak from the raft, showing off as usual. He hadn't said hello to her but she caught him watching her once.

Anyway, she and Bitsy had gone off into the bay to sit on their log. A creek came out there, smelling musty and edged with brown sap from the trees. A beech willow drooped above their heads and in a semicircle around them grew wild, fragile, mauve irises. She and Bitsy hadn't picked any irises knowing they would die right away. They just sat there digging their toes into the cool, damp sand and drawing patterns in the sand with sticks.

The week before, she and Bitsy had been walking up the track on their way home from school when they saw a thing like a transparent balloon lying flaccid on one of the ties. It was wet looking, and when Anna squatted to see, she noticed a milky liquid had seeped from the balloon. It smelled swampy and sort of unpleasant. She reached out.

"Don't touch it!" Anna jumped. Bitsy never gave orders; in fact Bitsy didn't talk much at all.

"Why not?"

"Don't you know what it is?"

Anna shook her head. Bitsy got a guilty little smirk on her face. "Tell me, Bitsy!"

"It's the thing men put on when they stick their doohickeys in women to make babies."

"Cheese and crust, what are you talking about?"

For once Bitsy had the upper hand and she was going to hold it as long as she could. "Don't you know anything, Anna?"

"Tell me before I give you a good smack, Bitsy."

Bitsy gave a theatrical sigh. "Well, babies grow in ladies' stomachs."

"Well I know that. First the ladies walk around as big as boulders and then babies come. I think it's sort of gross."

"Not as gross as the way they get in there."

"Tell."

So Bitsy told.

"I don't believe it. Are you trying to tell me that my Daddy used to stick his doohickey into my Mumma? They would never do that." Shame engulfed her. She looked down at the balloon and her stomach churned.

"It's true."

"Swear by St. Anthony?"

"I swear."

"Double swear?"

"Double swear!"

Now sitting on the log, Anna was seized with a terrible throat clenching brain-swimming need to talk about this mystery. She whispered instinctively and so did Bitsy, as if one of the guilty adults who did this ugly stuff might overhear.

"Do you think they look at each other without their clothes on?" Anna asked.

"I guess when they have to unless they close their eyes."

"I wonder if it hurts the ladies."

"My big sister says that they really like doing it and that they make lots of noise."

A shivering began between Anna's thighs. A tremor ran up one edge of her body and down the other. She wanted to touch herself. Instead, she opened her legs and pointed at the crotch of her pink bathing suit. "They do it there, don't they? I wonder what it feels like. Bitsy put your hand on me there."

Bitsy jumped up. "No."

"Okay, don't get scared." Anna put her own hand between her legs and began to rub. A wonderful tingling suffused her, and all the juices of her body rushed to the place she was rubbing and gathered in a searing point of pleasure. "Oh, Bitsy, it feels so good. Do it to yourself." Bitsy wouldn't but she sat down again.

The good feeling came to an apex and faded. "What if we let a boy touch us?"

"It would be a mortal sin."

"But what if he was a big boy and he kidnapped us and told us he would kill us if we didn't take off all our clothes and let him look. It wouldn't be a sin if we did it. Anyway I would put three roses on me, two on my chest and one down there. "

Bitsy's face was very red. "I guess we'd have to do it."

"Yes. And if he made us let him pick the roses and put his hand down between our legs, we couldn't help it. It wouldn't be a sin."

"What if he put his doohickey in us."

"Criminy custard, Bitsy. Don't get sickening."

Anna didn't masturbate again for a year but during that time she had to go with a bunch of kids in a car from the beach to the ferry, because it was raining buckets. One of the boys sat squished between her and another girl, and he leaned forward to get room. His bare, tanned back stretched vulnerable, young muscles taught and warm. Anna longed to run her hands over him. The next day when she lay on her bed reading a book from the library, she rolled over on her tummy and put her hand down between her legs and stroke herself until she gasped and shuddered. It became something she could not do without. She knew she was committing a mortal sin and she would go straight to hell, but she couldn't stop. And no way on earth could she tell it in confession. It was too horrible to contemplate. So she made bad confessions for three years, each time damning herself anew.

It was during a religious retreat when the grade nines were bused to Ottawa where they were locked up in a retreat house with a lot of French nuns who wore white habits and never spoke and didn't allow you to speak not even at meals. Anna had decided after years of sin to confess to the handsome young missionary retreat master who preached like a Jesuit who understood kids. She awoke in her room at sunrise, dressed, and sat in the window watching the world come alive. Terrified. Today she would confess. Then she retreated into her inner world.

As she rose in chapel to go to communion, the universe went black. She woke to find ugly Sister St. Mathilda gazing down at her. She was in a coffin. No she was looking up at the underside of a pew.

"Am I dead, Sister?"

"No, Anna."

Later that day, Anna confessed to the handsome young missionary priest. He said, "Ask Jesus to forgive you, child and try not to sin again. For your penance say a decade of your beads."

"It was that easy?" Anna decided that the whole idea of sin was not what she had been told. Perhaps the only way of truly sinning was to hurt others and not be sorry afterward?

When, a few years later, she sinned the biggest sin of all, she felt no guilt. It was Mumma who heard her confession and when she told Mumma what she had to do and the whole family was in an uproar, Mumma decided.

"Anna will make up her own mind," she said.

Anna also made up her mind about Aunt Beverly. And learned that all children were not as cherished as Anna herself was. Her little cousin, Emma, had always been a solitary child with a frantic need to be loved. Beverly was incapable of giving that love, but instead vented her twisted anger on the child. She never actually beat her; Nana Jeanne would have turned her out and kept the child; but Beverly's relentless, merciless tongue battered and belittled while the little girl with the large, silent, deep water blue eyes stood carved in marble. Nana was not a demonstrative person so Emma turned to her cousins and her Aunt Faith.

One summer's day, she came running up the path to Faith's front porch. She was six years old. Faith and Anna were sitting on the porch step, a favourite perch. Faith, new wire-rimmed spectacles perched on the end of her turned-up nose, was reading an Emily Loring romance and Anna a Sherlock Holmes detective story. They both looked up at once. Emma stood staring at them. Her still baby plump body was shaking uncontrollably and her white shoes with their rounded toes and single cross straps danced up and down with a life of their own. She was perspiring, but her face was whiter than Anna had ever seen anyone's.

"What is it, Child?" Faith was down the steps with Emma in her arms before Anna could move.

It took long minutes of coaxing and soothing before Emma could speak, and when she did, the story came out in jagged chunks, like ice being chipped from a block. It seemed that one of Beverly's men friends had come to call driving a new Ford automobile. While he sipped lemonade in the summer kitchen with Beverly, the little boy from next door came over to admire the car.

He said to Emma who was sitting lonesome on the back step, "I know a joke you could play that would make everybody laugh."

Emma, who had been born trusting even the mean, decided that to make her mother's friend laugh would make her mother happy, too.

The mean boy showed her that the man had left his keys in the car's ignition. "It would be a really funny joke if you locked all the doors." Emma obeyed, already feeling a wee bit uncomfortable but still trusting. Then she hid in the back shed to see the joke's outcome.

The man was furious. Mother cried, and terrified Emma ran around behind Nana's log house and down the street to Aunt Faith's who got the story out of her and said, "Now no gentleman would blame an innocent child for a prank instigated by that bad little Mercer boy. I shall march right over there and set this right. You take charge of Emma, Anna"

Anna took the child into the kitchen and onto her knee in the green rocking chair and told her the story of the *Borrowers* who lived in the walls of her house and borrowed things to make their own snug rooms behind the baseboards. "They use empty thread spools for tables and sit on bolt nuts. They hang their thimble pots on hairpins over their cooking fire and sleep in matchbox beds." All this from a book Mumma had bought her.

Emma stared at her, absolute belief in the enormous blue eyes.

Mumma came back in no time to tell Emma, "The gentleman is not angry at you at all, though Henry Mercer got a good scolding. In fact, the keys were retrieved with the help of a wire hanger, and your Mother is going off with her friend to dinner at the Dunkeld Hotel. You are to spend the night here."

Emma flew at Faith and gave her a mighty hug, in the process knocking off her new spectacles and breaking them. Before either Anna or Faith could react, she was out the back door and running to hide in the tall weeds beyond Faith's garden.

Faith said, "Leave her be, Anna." And sure enough the child tiptoed on her little white shoes back to the kitchen at supper time.

Another time, Emma accidentally spilled her picture painting water into the sink on top of some thawing meat. Convinced she would be poisoned, she ate the meat at supper anyway and lay awake all night waiting to die. It was weeks before she confided in Anna.

Anna wanted only to protect this sensitive, vulnerable child, and she did all a twelve-year-old could do. She even yelled at Aunt Beverly once and told her she was an old witch. Mumma's punishment for this sin was so mild that Anna suspected she agreed with her.

Chapter 14

EMMA

Winter 1960

Anna loves walking in the back meadow at Dunkeld House when she is bundled up and it's just cold enough to make her cheeks burn though her body and feet are toasty warm. Today the sun is concealed behind milk glass but still spreads soft light on the snow. She steps in a gopher hole and jars her young bones. But her lungs feel like billowing sails, and she only half resents the other wanderer who has already written on the purity of the snow in her back meadow.

Bridget's Golden Retriever, Fergus, a curly-haired giant purchased to protect Dunkeld house from the likes of Old Man Logan, walks guard beside her. Anna's little Sheltie, Pansy, is too short to plow through deep snow and sits in matronly dignity in front of the kitchen fireplace at home, that is, if she hasn't toddled up the kitchen stairs to lie at Faith's feet.

Fergus tears off in his usual patterns, sniffing in delight the trace left by the other walker, a figure seen always at a distance, quicker, perhaps younger than Anna. Fergus looks back both to be sure Anna is coming and to make certain she doesn't catch up. Then he comes thundering back like a wild Palomino pony, straight for her, an equine beast who swerves around her at the last moment and then tears off grinning. He takes their usual path along the uniform windbreak of firs with underskirts cut off, like a bunch of conical convent boarders promenading in a row.

The snow lies thinner under the trees and Anna compares her footprints to those of the other solitary walker. Hers are smaller and she can move under the trees without hitting her head whereas his prints swerve outwards and then back. She and Fergus do their thing and then come back along the same trail. Fergus decides he's had enough and takes the path for home, looking back to see if Anna is going to cooperate. She does. But first she must stop and stare at the trees which surround Dunkeld House.

My tall, tall cedars which would look prissy if they weren't so old. Midnight green. My oaks stand stately and unapproachable. My naked apple trees to the west. My two huge poplars arrogantly point all their branches at the sky, except those arms severed by last year's ice storm. From here my trees look like artist's background, but when I come under them they soar. How can any tree climb so high and not fall down? The poplars stand bare, not like the willow up the way, just as old and even bigger, which droops with yellow ochre strands like an elderly lady who had lost her petticoats and hangs herself with threads.

Anna enters Dunkeld House by way of the back pillared colonnade and comes thankful into the warmth. Fergus trots down the long hall and turns left into the kitchen. She follows leaving gobs of snow on the slate floor laid by Great Grampa Angus himself. The kitchen flickers with orange and red reflections from the fire. Nana's mantle clock ticks loudly in the silence. Fergus goes through his ritual of drinking too much water too quickly and then throws up his lunch on the kitchen floor.

Will I ever learn to empty the water bowl before we go out?

Anna removes her boots and bundling and puts them near the fire to dry and she has just cleaned up Fergus's mess when the kitchen door jerks open and Rachel stumbles in. She is wearing fur-topped boots and a tightly waisted, brown, flared coat that conceals the uniform she loves. Her tam is sprightly though, a bright Kelly green knitted by Bridget and worn out of duty. It is a chilly walk from the foot of the drive where the school bus lets her off, especially when the wind is gusting off the bay. Her cheeks are crimson with whitish spots, and her coppery hair frizzes from her shoulders as if dancing with cold.

But her eyes.

"What is it? What's wrong?"

Rachel bursts into tears. "Oh Mother, if only I had known sooner. I knew she was drinking beer and running around with the hoods but …"

"Rachel! What are you jabbering about?"

"It's Emma."

Terror inside.

"She's run away with one of those hoods. Mary Flaherty's big sister saw them getting on the Colonial Coach. She had a knapsack. She's gone."

"Don't' be ridiculous!" Why am I shouting at Rachel? She's just a little girl. "Emma would never …"

"I'm sorry. I'm sorry," Rachel cries.

"Don't. Don't, child. It's not your fault. You had nothing to do with it."

"I should have told before."

Sudden calm. She puts her arms around her daughter. "No, Dear Heart, I knew. I should have stopped her." Would I have? "Did Mary say she went with a boy?"

Rachel murmurs into her shoulder. "Yes. He …"

"I don't want to know who he is."

When Rachel has cried herself dry, Anna makes her a cup of tea and climbs the stairs to Mumma's room. Faith and Pansy are watching the top of the stairs. Faith will know, always knows. She lifts a thin hand and holds it out towards Anna.

"Come sit by me," she says.

Ann sits on the old quilt. Faith stitched it as a girl. In its center, a doll-faced girl in a pink hoop-skirt holds a basket of bluebells, bleeding hearts, and purple delphinium. More flowers bloom around her feet and bluebirds fly about her head. Anna smoothes Faith's pillows.

"It's Emma," she says.

Faith nods, calm sadness in her grey-blue eyes.

"She's run off, with a boy I think."

Faith nods again.

"There's more."

"There is always more, Anna."

A long silence.

"There'll be hell to pay."

Faith smiles.

Anna sighs. "I know. We have to let her go."

Chapter 15

CHARLIE

1961

Anna and Colleen are walking down Main Street. It hasn't changed a great deal since they were kids. The small Dunkeld Hotel needs white paint on its windows and double-tiered porches. The new post-office/town hall, a grand, pink quarried stone affair with a clock tower, dominates the eastern skyline. The grocery, the shoe store, the drugstore, Miss Doyle's hat shop, all brick fronted, the brand new movie house, a red-trimmed Woolworths, and two recently opened dress shops crowd the narrow street. The beer and liquor stores are hidden down by the Ottawa River, alongside a beer-parlour whose door decent folks do not darken. Joe Ching's Café, looking rundown, still squats beside the shoe shop, but the Astrolabe Café is long gone. The teens have given their allegiance to a burger place on the edge of the village. The teen's themselves look as if dressed for alternative costume parties. The daughters of the doctors and dentists and decent folk wear pastel Crimplene blouses with three quarter length sleeves and straight skirts which make them look like coloured pencils with breasts, or sunburst plaid reversible skirts which make them look big-assed. Under these skirts are elastic panty girdles and bare shaved legs reaching down to white socks and white bucks or saddle shoes. Some of the luckier girls have purloined their boyfriend's or older brother's fishermen knit sweaters. These maidens are universally humped over burdens composed of binders and books of many colours. A lot of them have cut off their fifties' ponytails, and hairdos vary from ugly short with spiral curls on the forehead to long and silky.

These girls are accompanied or followed by boys in jeans and T-shirts. In contrast to these respectable types are the girls in tight-as-can-be skirts or too-short shorts and summer sweaters under which their breasts are molded into cones; their consorts, the true rebels, sport greased down duck-tail haircuts, second skin jeans and, even in the springtime heat, black leather jackets. Three of these lads gyrate along side by side. They are the village gang who call themselves the Wanderers. Unfortunately, none of the gang spells very well, so the name emblazoned on the back of their leather jackets is the *Wanders.*

Anna's heart tightens. Emma had gone off with the fourth member of the Wanders. *God help all children.*

A gaggle of Convent girls sail by in antiquated black uniforms. They do not deign to glance at the rest of their age group. Anna prefers the hoods. Though she rather likes the long, loose hair on the Convent girls. Even her own little Rachel wears her titian glory in a thick braid down her back. Hair has become a way of expressing oneself. Colleen's fair curls have been whipped into kinks and waves held together by some sort of blue goo. Anna's own brown thicket floats around her head in disarray. Perhaps she should wear a velvet headband like Emma.

Emma.

Anna doesn't notice the man until he is standing in front of her.

"Well, if it isn't the Dunkeld girls." He isn't tall or short but average. He has broad shoulders, a thick muscular neck and small hips, and brown straight hair worn just a little longer than older men's. His skin is an even bronze, whether from sun or heredity is a puzzle. He is wearing dress pants and a short-sleeved yellow shirt. His sparkling blue eyes laugh as he reaches for Colleen and then Anna and kisses them firmly on their cheeks. Colleen blushes.

"Mygod, Charlie Stuart!" Anna is surprised at the sudden warmth that zings from the top of her head to the tip of her toenails. "I thought you were away at Toronto University."

"I graduated. I am now an official lawyer working for Old Lawyer Smith. God it's good to see you both."

"How is your mother?" Anna asked. "I always liked her."

"She is well, as solitary as ever.

"I hear you are at Dunkeld House now. The little grey house across from my mother's looks lonely."

"Yes the whole clan moved some time ago."

"How are they all?"

"You know about Aunt Beverly and Mumma?"

"Yes, Mother told me. It's too bad. You know I used to hike across your land last winter during breaks and look at the old place."

"You were the mysterious walker? Why didn't you drop in?"

"I should have. Hey you girls want to stop in at Joe's for coffee?"

Colleen says, "We're shopping, Charlie." Anna knows she is afraid he will ask about Emma or her own failed marriage.

"Nonsense. You finish the shopping, Colleen. I want to talk to Charlie."

They sit at the smart aleck boys' table. They are gone now. Some still around town, never amounting to much, others suddenly grown sensible and gone off to universities and careers. Joe's place is exactly the same with country-girl waitresses and even Joe, himself, behind the cash register. He comes over to their table and nods and bobs and smiles. He has grey hair around a bald spot but his face is still a firm round button.

"Hi, Joe," Charlie says.

Anna smiles, afraid that she is going to cry from nostalgia. She weeps too easily lately. "Do you still have Tin Roofs?" she asks.

"I make." And Joe goes behind the counter and emerges quickly with two Tin Roofs. Anna's mouth waters just as it always did.

"Joe's treat."

They thank him and he goes away.

"Sweet-god-in-heaven, it's good to see you Charlie. Do you remember how we used to play under the hedge?" This brings on a flood of memory-talk including the sleigh ride at the Holy Roller Church. They slide inevitably into fond silence.

Charlie's face turns serious. "I heard about all your trouble, Anna. I'm sorry." And she can tell he really is.

"I'm all right, Charlie. And how about you? Got a girl?"

Charlie grins. "Had a few at college. But you can't beat the girls of Dunkeld Village. I'm still in love with the little brat from across the street."

"Go way with you. A lawyer is it?" He nods. "You always were the smartest boy in town. And I know who I'll go to if I need help." His lean face is suddenly concerned, so much like the old Charlie who used to give his friend sound advice which she never took.

He takes her hands in his warm paws. "Anna, I mean it when I say that if there is ever anything, ANYTHING, I can do for you, I will be mad as hell if you don't come to me."

Sudden tears again sting her eyes. "I know that, Charlie." The years have fallen away and her friend is here again. She savours the old comfortable, safe feeling she always knew with Charlie.

They part on the sidewalk promising to meet, knowing they probably won't except in passing. Anna strides across the street heading for Bishop's Ladies Wear where she knows that Colleen will be drooling over the latest summer fashion, shift dresses. Colleen who is always so beautifully dressed even on a slim budget. Anna turns to look back. Charlie is standing watching her. She waves and walks away smiling.

Autumn comes with its wonderful crisp as starch days, air clear and water-sweet, nights before early fires. Anna is sitting on the ground under her apple trees when she notices the hood coming up the drive. Louis steps like a shadow from the stable and stops the lad. They talk and Louis comes over to Anna. She puts back in her basket the MacIntosh she has been about to bite.

"There's a lad wants to talk to you," Louis says. His face is as expressionless as always but there is something in the way he stands.

Anna rises brushing leaves from her apron, the tangy smell of apples following her. As she draws closer to him, she recognizes the Wander who went away with Emma. He looks the worse for wear, emaciated but clean. His freckled face is pale and his hands shake. His leather jacket has seen better days.

The Watcher inside would like to see if the name *Wanders* is still emblazoned on his back.

"You're one of the Baker lads, aren't you?"

"Yeah."

"You used to chum around with Emma."

Silence.

"What can I do for you?"

"Well, you see, it's about Emma." No. No. "I thought I should … you should know …"

"Is she all right?"

"Yeah, I mean for now. It's just that she's in with a bad crowd. The rest of us from the Valley stayed together but Emma … she just seems to want to punish herself or something."

"Drugs?"

"Yeah and bad goings on. I wouldn't tell on her but Emma's a good kid. You got to try to stop her, Mrs. Dunkeld."

Anna asks him in for hot chocolate but he refuses, apologizes over and over again for bothering her, and starts to leave after telling her that he doesn't really know where Emma is except that she hasn't left Ottawa, as far as he knows, but that she might be taking off for Vancouver soon.

He is turning away when he remembers something. He drops his pack on the ground and rummages through it. He comes up with a dusty black velvet box. "Emma said to give you this if I saw you." Anna doesn't have to open the box to know it contains the Dunkeld broach.

"What shall I do, Cousin Bridget? I can't go off and leave you alone with your bad legs to care for Mumma and Beverly and Rachel, even with Colleen to help. And I wouldn't know where or how to look for Emma." They are in Bridget's sitting room just off the big bedroom she shares with Louis. It was once a nursery for Angus Dunkeld's children. The logs are lit in the ornate fireplace, twin to the one in the library below. Bridget rocks back and forth in her old oak rocker plumped with cushions decorated with unlikely purple peonies.

"Doesn't seem there is much you can do, child." She still thinks of Anna as approaching adulthood, though Anna is older that Bridget herself was on the blazing summer's day when she had helped deliver her. "Louis would go."

Anna knows just how much help and respect a Métis would receive in Ottawa, even from the police. She shakes her head.

She heaves a sigh and straightens her aching back. "I am going to ask Charlie."

Charlie Stuart drops everything, climbs into his old Austin and takes off for Ottawa that very evening.

Charlie spends a week in Ottawa, staying in the YMCA and walking day and night the Byward Market, Rideau Street, Vanier, and Hull, questioning teens and the proprietors of cafes and bars. He finds some kids from Eganville and Pembroke but none of them know Emma or have met anyone like her. The police say that she has probably hitchhiked West but they will keep an eye out. He leaves with them a photograph of Emma in her convent uniform.

Anna knows when the Austin pulls up at the kitchen door, and before Charlie comes sad-faced into the house, that Emma is gone.

BOOK II

Chapter 16

DUNKELD HOUSE

1950

Uncle Patrick's frail heart gave out during the autumn of 1949, and his friend Bill came to town for the funeral at the white church.

"We shall walk up the center isle on either side of Bill," Nana said to Beverly.

"I will not walk beside that man. He is unnatural."

Anna liked Bill who is gentle and self-effacing like Uncle Patrick had been. "I'll walk with you, Nana Jeanne," she declared.

"As will I," said Mumma.

Nana Jeanne said in a trembly voice, "You, Anna, and you, Faith, are true Dunkelds."

Nana died the following year but not before she had told Anna all about Dunkeld House. Anna didn't let on that she had already heard most of it from Richard.

"You see, the first Dunkeld House was in Ayrshire, Scotland. Your great grandfather, Angus Dunkeld, left it to come to Canada. He worked like a slave in the lumber shanties and he established this village. He became a rich man with a hotel, a livery stable, and three farms. He sent his sons to university in Ottawa. My Poor Sean was an engineer."

"Did Angus own Dunkeld Hotel?" Anna asked, referring to the old building on Main Street.

"Yes, but you understand it does not belong to us now. We are poor now. Angus lost everything when the railroad came through and the lumbermen moved west and no longer needed the produce he freighted to them from his farms, nor did they need his hotel. He sold all but the home farm where I lived with Poor Sean until the old folks died, that would be Angus and the second wife. She was an Algonquin Indian, you know, but a real beauty. Your great grandmother was as Irish as Paddy's pig and a wee bit fey."

Anna's eyes grew enormous but she kept her mouth shut. Nana did not like being interrupted.

"Grandpa Sean let out Dunkeld House when the old folks died."

Anna's decision to be silent, faltered. "Do we still own it? Where is it?"

"You know how in the west end of the village there's a bridge across the opening to Dunkeld Bay?" Anna had never gone on her own beyond that bridge and had done no exploring along the shores of the bay. "Well, there's a dirt road going in there beside a mixed forest. Great Grampa Angus would never let them cut those trees. Some of them are a hundred years old. Well, down that road a couple of miles is Dunkeld House. It's a shabby now, so the rent I get is low, but it serves quite well as a rooming house for those less fortunate than we. The town keeps up the road even in winter because they have plans for the bay."

"You mean we own this house? Is it a mansion?"

The Watcher inside said sarcastically, *"Do dreams come true?"*

"I own it and it would have gone to your father along with a little income to pay the taxes."

"Cheese and crust!"

"Don't be vulgar, Anna."

That Saturday afternoon Anna inveigled Bitsy into a long walk to Dunkeld House. After crossing the steel bridge over the creek that joined the bay and the Ottawa River, they strolled down a dirt road with tree branches forming a protective arch far above. This was real forest like in the fairy tales. Surely trolls and goblins and ogres lurked just out of sight. Anna and Bitsy stood on either side of an oak and tried to join hands. It would have taken four girls to do it. They had to be satisfied with picking up acorns and scratching happy faces on them.

"Don't you just love this place?" Anna shouted, running down the road and then twirling with her arms extended and her wild hair flying. She could smell the furniture odour of pines, but also the nutty fragrance of oaks, and maples' and birches' clean tang. There were raspberry bushes along the roadside but they didn't hold any berries, probably because of the deep shade.

Anna fled singing and shouting at the top of her lungs.

> *He wore a tourie on his bonnet, a red tourie on it*
> *A red tourie, ourie, ourie eh.*
> *He left his kilt in Scorrin, and off he went to war in*
> *His red tourie, ourie, ourie eh.*
> *Now when swinging into action, he's the center of attraction*
> *He's the pride of bonny Scotland, so they say*
> *But what made the Gerries run?*
> *It was not his tommy gun*
> *'Twas the tourie on his bonnet*
> *The bonny tourie on it*
> *The red tourie, ourie, ourie, eh.*

Bitsy followed silently, hitting the ground with a switch.

Anna looked back. She thinks I'm crazy. Well, maybe I am.

She began to think about Nana Jeanne. Nana had told her she was going to die a few days before she actually did. "And I don't want you mourning, child. Don't forget me and grow up to be a fine, decent woman, and I shall watch over you if the Good Lord allows it. Mind your Mother. Keep Richard alive in your heart. And look out for Emma."

Anna had promised. She wept, of course, but always felt that Nana had her eye on her and didn't much appreciate the tears. She put pussy willows she had dried that spring on Nana Jeanne's grave.

She came around a curve, and the waters of Dunkeld Bay twinkled on her left and to the right on a rise, a beautiful old house stood. It was big and rectangular with a deeply recessed entrance on its front. It had been built with quarried stone walls that stood strong as ever with neglected Ivy trailing all the way to the roof. Many-paned, tall windows caught the sunshine and no less than two chimneys towered at either end of the house. The open space around looked neglected but the stables to one side were in good shape, though the wood had been allowed to weather to a soft, shimmering grey. Ancient trees rustled everywhere but not crowding in on the house, instead standing back as if to say, "We are the setting for this sombre jewel."

There were a couple of rattletrap cars parked near the stables but no people. An elderly border collie sauntered over to Anna and sniffed her shoes and legs, his tail wagging.

"Good boy. Oh come on, Bitsy. This dog wouldn't harm an ant."

The Watcher inside said, *"This is your belonging place."*

Anna marched up to the entrance to Dunkeld House. A solid oak door with iron fittings was enclosed in a deep porch. The door squeaked ajar. She pushed it. It moved easily. Great Grandfather Dunkeld had built well. Anna went inside.

The central hallway was immense with walnut wainscoting reaching to the ceiling. There were three double doors, all closed, on either side; at the end of the hallway a wide staircase led up, up to one of the tall, many-paned windows. Anna climbed the stairs. *I have been here before, but when?* The graceful, wide banister felt familiar, homely, under her hand. When she reached the top, Anna looked out the window at beaver meadows with forest beyond.

She longed to open all the double doors off the upper hall, which formed a T-shape with the gallery, but Nana Jeanne would not have approved and Mumma would have said, "There are people living here, Anna."

Well someone was taking care of Anna's house. The wood shone and the slate floors in the hallway below had been recently scrubbed. She would thank that person some day and for now … She went back down and out to Bitsy.

"Now why didn't you come in?"

Bitsy dug a hole in the dirt with the tip of her black running shoe.

They spent the rest of the afternoon playing along the bay's shore. Dunkeld House watched as if waking from a spell.

Chapter 17

SIMPLICITY

1963

Anna is lounging on her favourite chair in the shade of the porticoed back terrace of Dunkeld House. Dickens's *Dombey and Son* lies face down in her lap. Nothing soothes like Dickens. She takes a sip from the crystal glass on the wrought iron table near her elbow. German Riesling, happiness on the tongue. It's her twenty-sixth birthday. Tonight the family will produce the obligatory cake and thoughtful gifts but for now she prefers to be alone, Mumma and Beverly safely asleep, the twins playing house with Rachel in the meadow. She can see their bright heads bobbing like people flowers among the tall, distant grasses.

That morning she had ushered a grimy Jimmy into the bathroom and filled the sink with warm soapy water.

"Don't wash me!" Tootsie's twin, Jimmy, had wailed.

"Don't be ridiculous, Jimmy. You are absolutely filthy."

"Please, please don't wash me."

"Why ever not, child?"

"My dirt keeps me warm."

Both Tootsie and Jimmy are adorable, innocent, and unimaginative. Once Tootsie broke one of Faith's knitting needles and the two of them wadded a yard of cellophane tape around the break, absolutely convinced that no one would notice. The world exists for their pleasure. The whole family spoils them. Rachel spent hours making a doll house for Tootsie out of a cardboard shoe box with furniture and people cut from the Eaton's catalogue. Anna herself has built many a tinker-toy structure with Jimmy.

They take it all as their due. Nothing phases them. They will go far in this world. Too bad their mother can't share in their invulnerability.

Above her and around the green, green lawn, which Louis keeps silky and fragrant, the oaks and poplars stand guard, summer wind rustling like crinolines through the poplar leaves. Anna loves that sound.

"We have done all right by Dunkeld House, have we not, Great Grandfather Angus?" she says aloud, remembering that first day when they arrived with only a root from Nana's lilac trees, Faith's yellow rose bush, and a few pieces of furniture. Nana had left Dunkeld House to Anna; Faith needed special care; Cousin Bridget offered to nurse her; and someone had to look after Beverly and provide a home for Colleen and the twins. It was decided to give up all the smaller houses and move en masse to Dunkeld House. Anna was scared and excited at the same time. They pooled what money they had, and went home. The house gathered them in. There were a lot of shabby antiques left behind by Great Grandfather Angus. And books. And in no time the family was settled as if they had never left.

In truth, things have gradually smoothed out financially. Between them, Anna and Louis, with the help of the Wander who once ran away with Emma, handle the house and grounds upkeep. Bridget and Colleen see that the rooms are vacuumed and polished to a prideful degree. And they do most of the cooking. Rachel, in her little-old-lady way, is wonderful with the twins. Everyone nurses Mumma and they take turns walking Beverly through the grounds and the orchards. Beverly no longer speaks to anyone but her body remains strong. Her face is a wondering child's. Anna still brings her a chocolate bar every day and she is getting softly plump.

Anna closes her eyes. She doesn't hear Colleen trot down the central hall and is aware of her only as a dream presence until she touches her shoulder.

"Anna. Anna? Wake up. You will never guess who is at the front door."

"Who? What?"

"No. You must come and see" and Colleen hurries back into the house.

"Criminy Custard."Anna struggles from her chair, rubs her eyes, smoothes her blue peddle pushers. "God. I hope it isn't the priest trying to get Colleen to go back to Hank. No, she wouldn't have come for me. Cheese and Crust. Maybe it's the Presbyterian minister come to save me after all these years."

The hallway is long, cool, its only light sunshine slanting through stained glass on either side of the front door. A figure stands in shadow. Anna peers at it, moving quickly forwards. A tiny, stalwart woman with a determined stance and an out of date house-dress. She is wearing red running shoes and her mousy hair sits on top of her head like a muddy doughnut. Anna rushes forward, arms open.

"Bitsy!"

Bitsy allows the hug, ignores the flood of questions, waits for Anna to shut up and then says, "I am here on important business and there are those who need your help, Anna Dunkeld!"

Can this be shy, timorous, silent Bitsy? Anna knows she married a Douglas area farmer and they are doing well, raising corn and wheat and a large brood of children, but they seldom come to Dunkeld Village.

"Shall we go sit in the kitchen? It is cool in there with the breeze off the bay." Bitsy agrees, marches into the kitchen, and plumps her round bottom into Mumma's green rocking chair. "Can I offer you a Coke or some juice?"

"No thank you, Anna. As I said, I have something important to discuss with you."

Anna backs into a chair and sits.

"Promise me you will not interrupt until you have heard me out."

"I promise." She wants to add, *Cross my heart and hope to die.* But Bitsy never did have much sense of humour.

"I brought the truck. It's out back and in it is a very sadly abused girl." Bitsy glares as if daring Anna to interrupt. "This girl, whose name is Mary O'Rourke, is a motherless young woman who keeps house for her worthless brothers and drunken father over on Mount Saint Patrick. The long and short of it is, the girl has been misused for years; she got pregnant, God only knows by whom, and the pigs have thrown her out. She's a good Catholic girl so she will have the child. I would take her in but I haven't the room or time to take proper care of her. I want you to keep her here until her baby is born then my husband and I will take her to the city and help her find a job. It's up to her whether she keeps the child. That's the long and short of it." Bitsy closes her mouth over the longest speech Anna has ever heard her make.

God Almighty, do I have to take care of the whole world? "You want me to keep her here at Dunkeld House?" A thousand reasons why not skip through Anna's head.

"That's what I said. Tess will take over her medical care. I already spoke to her."

Tess Sauvé has just completed her internship in an Ottawa Hospital and, to Anna's delighted surprise, has come to set up general practice in Dunkeld Village. In fact, her office sign is out on Main Street and the last Anna heard she is busy moving into one of the new classy apartments on Dover Street.

"Well?" Bitsy says quietly.

"Don't leave the poor girl sitting in that hot truck any longer. Let's go get her." Bridget will kill me. Rachel will be jealous. "Better still, you bring her in and I'll pour a nice cold glass of milk for her."

Mary O'Rourke is a sweaty-faced slip of a thing with the eyes of a koala bear. When Bitsy tells her she is to stay with Anna, she starts to cry, rocking in the vacated green rocking chair holding her stomach like a brown cotton basketball in her lap. They coax her to drink the milk, guide her up the big polished staircase and put her to bed in the spare room beside Anna's.

As soon as, mission done, Bitsy has disappeared in a cloud of dust down the road, Anna is on the phone to Charlie. He, being Charlie, gives a lot of free lawyerly advice the upshot of which is that Mary is over eighteen, can live where she likes and with whom she likes. If the male O'Rourkes, an unlikely event according to Charlie, decide to force her home, they can be slapped with a restraining order.

Mary, despite the big stomach, proves to be a tough little biscuit. She doesn't talk much, probably has never been allowed to, but she is healthy, peppy, and mild-mannered, is generous with her shy smiles and insists upon working at any task that presents itself, to earn her keep. The twins fall immediately in love with her because she plays dolls with Tootsie and draws horses for Jimmy. Faith finds her presence soothing and the pregnant girl can often be found sitting by the invalid's side, usually knitting something pink, while Faith dreams away the long summer days. Colleen, though shocked by Mary's *unfortunate condition,* is distantly kind. Rachel develops a grudging respect for Mary's pluck and spends a lot of time watching television with her in the evenings. Strangely enough they like the Saturday night hockey games best and almost have conniption fits when Gordie Howe scores his five hundred and forty-fifth goal.

The first house call Tess makes to see Mary, sees her also checking out Mumma's lungs, Bridget's rheumatic joints, and the twins' ears. With

Tess's frequent, calm presence in the house, Anna feels some of the load slip from her shoulders and somehow thinks she will make it after all.

"I love your hair that way, Tess."

They are sitting near the Ottawa River on the village dock, watching the ferry come in, a favourite childhood pastime. The river is deep evening blue and choppy. A saucy wind blows down the Valley. Érable Island lies serene in the distance. Up to now they have been silent.

The aforementioned hair hangs in a thick black braid down Tess's graceful back. It has the wonderful dark glow of most native hair. Tess is a beauty like her mother before her but when asked if there are any men in her life, she smiles quietly and shrugs.

"What about you, Anna?"

"It's too much trouble. I've had a few brief flings now that we have the pill but I've never again felt that desperate, all consuming crazy passion I had with Rachel's father and of course, poor old Ken …"

"Did you have much trouble getting the pill?"

Anna laughs. "The Valley doctors are still not sure of its legality unless you are bleeding up a storm or something. I went to the city."

The ferry chugs into dock and a couple of cars are jockeyed off, a few tired families with picnic baskets trudge onto the dock and then the island people with their town purchases get on. Anna remembers four little girls boarding the ferry for longed-for picnics on the island.

"Whatever happened to Ruby Flaherty?" Tess asks, reading Anna's mind as she always has.

"She married a soldier, believe it or not. I think she's in Camp Borden. Colleen gets letters from her."

"And Colleen? She seems unhappy."

"She is. For some crazy reason she still loves that beast she married. He beat the shit out of her every chance he got and then would cry and beg forgiveness. I hate his guts."

"Any danger of her going back to him?"

"No. He married a little Polish girl from Killaloe. From what I hear he has met his match. She'd break his neck if he lifted a finger and she has five huge brothers to back her up."

Tess grins.

"And how about you? Are you glad you came back to Dunkeld?"Anna asks.

Tess folds her arms across her chest and rubs them as if she were cold. "It's as good as anywhere."

Anna decides to plunge. "Look, slap me down if I'm out of line but is being Algonquin still as hard as it used to be? After all, you made it through med school and you seem to have a pretty good practice building."

Tess sighs. "There is no explaining it. You could never understand."

"The hell I can't. I'm no bigot."

"Of course not. But when you enter a public place, do you look around to see if hate is glancing your way? Do you cringe when a white man touches you no matter how innocently? Do you see drunken natives on the street and feel that they are somehow more disgusting than the white drunk leaning against them? Do friends ask you questions about what it's like to be white?"

Anna's Inner Voice scolds, *Birdbrain.* "I'm sorry. You're right."

"So let's talk about men."

"Let's not."

"And why not?"

"I don't like men."

"Of course you do. You and Louis are great friends."

"Anna. Grow up. I'm lesbian."

"Cheese and Crust!"

Tess starts to laugh. Anna starts to quiver then shake then howl. "Jesus, Mary and Joseph, what would Sister St. Timothy think?"

The Inner Voice asks, *What's wrong with me? Shouldn't I be shocked or something. In a book, this would be quite titillating. In real life, it's just Tess telling me something I probably knew all along, something that doesn't matter one bit. Oh but she must be unhappy. The Catholic Woman's League would crucify her if they knew. My dear, dear friend.*

"So what else is new?" she says. And they both break up again. Anna feels once more like a girl of seventeen, in her final year at Our Lady of Snows.

1954

The Grade Thirteen classroom was hot with the welcome, bone soothing warmth of spring. There were only six girls in the class so Sister St. Anthony allowed them to sprawl about. Two boarders were sitting on the windowsill through which they might, if a conflagration began, escape to the dubious safety of the upper verandah. Anna was studying Trigonometry. She hated

Trigonometry and Trigonometry hated her. Sister St. Anthony, wanting with all her heart for Anna to pass the Departmental Grade Thirteen Examinations, had coached her faithfully and exhaustively. In English, Anna shone. She had no rivals at the Convent of Our Lady of Snows and, in a school where Dickens and Shakespeare were still second only to Jesus and the Pope, Sister St. Anthony had singled her out. Two other girls were far smarter than Anna, one of them being Tess, and they had been pigeon-holed for scholarships to the Universities of Toronto or Ottawa. Anna would be patiently, exhaustively guided through her maths so she might be an English teacher and a writer.

Anna loved Sister St. Anthony. She was beautiful in every way. Her voice was soft and cultured. Her slim hands turned book pages with slow grace. Shakespearean sonnets flowed like holy wine from her lips. Her grey eyes filled with wonder as she spoke to them of Shelley, Robert Browning, T.S. Eliot, not that they were actually allowed to read T.S. Eliot who needed a mature mind. This maturity would seemingly be poured like balm upon Anna's brow when she got an A in English Literature. Sister St. Anthony was more than just kind and beautiful. She knew Anna. She saw into her soul. They spoke the same language. This cultured, brilliant nun had truly earned the name of Anna's favourite saint. And Anna wanted so much to please her.

One day a girl from Eganville, a girl Anna had met at a Retreat, invited her for the weekend. They were to go to a dance at Sunnydale Acres, where teenagers and young marrieds swung madly through square dances and clung together for romantic round dances. Anna was nervous about going to the dance. When she went to C.Y.O. dances in the Church basement in Dunkeld Village, she reverted to being fat and ugly. She knew she wasn't fat because she had gone down two dress sizes, but she felt fat. So she stood against a wall looking sulky and glaring about her as if expecting attack. The smart aleck girls danced with the smart aleck boys and the couples going steady cuddled disgustingly close until the younger of the two parish priests went over and said something jokingly into their ears, probably reminding them that there must be the length of a ruler between them at all times. This reminded Anna of Sister St. Ambrose in Grade Eight who told them that if they ever had to sit on a boy's lap, they were to put a book there first and sit on that. The upshot of it all was that hardly any boy asked Anna to dance and if one did, she was so silent and glum that she scared him off.

But tonight was different.

Anna looked at herself in the mirror. The new shirtwaist dress Mumma had bought her was a pretty shade of rose with tiny pleats and a row of pearl buttons on the bodice. This drew attention to her generous breasts, and the matching belt cinched in her small waist. The skirt was a floating cloud of rose and crinoline and Anna was wearing her first pair of white high heels. And she knew she had good legs. Mumma had told her so and Mumma did not lie.

"Don't tie your hair back. Anna," her new friend Greta said. You've got such lovely waves. Let it flow down your back.

Greta's parents drove them to the dance and would hang about as chaperones. It was very dark in the country and the lights shone from the dance hall doorways like lighthouse lanterns. It was only a clapboard rectangular building painted white but it drew cars and kids like minnows to dough balls. The fiddles and guitars were already riding the night air and couples had begun necking in dark cars. A group of boys swigged at a bottle in the shadows. They hid the bottle at Greta's parents' approach but they whistled at Anna and Greta.

They stepped into the dance hall. The loud pulse-hammering music buffeted them. The smell of perfume and sweat and whiskey breath and musk zinged into Anna's head making her dizzy.

"Let's go get a pop," Greta said. This was a good way to escape parents.

They walked to the wooden table where a man in a sodden white shirt was selling pop. Anna could feel eyes on her. She was a stranger here and thus exotic. All shyness fled. She looked boldly about. A boy with a dark curl hanging down over his eyes winked and made kissing motions with his lips. She looked away quickly but smiled. She could feel her cheeks getting hot.

She was asked to dance almost immediately by a gawky boy in a summer plaid sport shirt. Anna had seen him before while shopping in Pembroke, he hung about with the Presbyterian kids. He said his name was Kenneth Beck and he had just started work with his father in a Pembroke pharmacy. He was dour and frowned a lot, but he was also obviously smitten with Anna. It was a round dance and Kenneth stepped on her toes, but she was dancing, wasn't she? Then the caller shouted. "Grab your partners for a Square, lads!" And the fiddles began their gut-throbbing, foot-stomping rhythm.

Anna was sitting beside Greta's mother making polite conversation. A voice said, "Well, Miss Dunkeld, may I have the pleasure of this dance?"

It was Teddy Fisher.

He stood there radiating health and devilment. His curly red hair was tousled and sweaty. His body leaned over her, lithe and dangerous as a cougar. He smiled all over his face and his hazel eyes gleamed.

Anna's hand went out to meet his. It fit perfectly. He drew her to her feet and whispered in her ear. "Well, brat, you dress up real nice."

They danced until Anna's feet no longer touched the floor. He swung her through squares like she was an extension of his strong, freckled hands. His arm around her waist made her want to be held forever. He laughed as he lifted her off her feet. She was happy, happy, happy.

And then the lights were lowered and someone was crooning "Blue Moon" into the microphone. Teddy drew her close. His shirt was wet under her hand. She put her head down on his shoulder and he curled her other hand in his. He said her name and nothing else. He didn't try to push himself against her as some boys would but held her gently as if he thought she might shatter. Anna closed her eyes. They danced with no one else the rest of the evening.

When they played "Irene Goodnight" the signal for the dance's end, Teddy whispered, "Can I drive you home."

Dismay. "Oh I can't. I'm here with Greta's parents."

"I'm in the Airforce, Anna. I only get home about once a month. Can I write to you?"

"Yes."

And he did write, boyish letters full of big talk about how he would be an officer one day, a fly-boy. He never mentioned his mother or any other part of his life. Anna asked around. It seemed that Teddy drank too much and drove his red and white Chevy too fast. He was considered wild by the Valley girls. But he was true to his word. He came home on the first Saturday of the very next month. It was July. Anna had passed her departmental exams with respectable marks. Sister Anthony telephoned to tell her. Anna sent in her applications to University and knew she would be accepted because she would be highly recommended to St. Mikes, the Catholic College of the University of Toronto. But somehow the idea of going away to school had become less exciting.

Teddy took her to the movies. They saw James Dean *in Rebel Without a Cause.* Anna thought Teddy far more fascinating than James Dean. Afterwards they stopped for hamburgers on the edge of the village and Teddy drove her to a spot on the Ottawa River. The moon twinkled over the water. Anna could smell the river and the musk shaving lotion Teddy wore. When he took her in his arms, the kiss was warm and gentle. He didn't try to paw her. Only once the back of his hand softly moved across her breast. She was galvanized. She would have moved into his hands but he spoke.

"Anna. You aren't like other girls. I don't want us to be just a couple of idiots mucking about in the back seat of a car. You are too good for that."

"But Teddy. Don't you want me?"

He groaned. "I'm going to marry you, Anna. Don't say anything. Nothing."

They snuggled together looking out over the water, listening to the wind in the pines.

Their resolve lasted for one more visit. It was Anna's fault really. Her need for him had grown until nothing else mattered. She knew that this powerful bond had been formed between them as long ago as the time the mean boys had put wasps down his back. Teddy had been and was now the most fascinating male she had ever known. And with her he was special, all the crassness of his upbringing seemingly gone. She wanted him. She tempted him deliberately and when he gave in, she went to him with the open generosity of a grown woman. They laughed and they cried and they rose to heights not usually granted the young.

"I love you," he said.

And she answered, "I love you, too." As simple as that.

Chapter 18

TEDDY

1954

Anna is packing her trunk for St. Mikes. In it, liberally sprinkled with tears, are the second-hand first year English Literature texts which Miss McKrachen has found for her; her fancy skates; her essays from Grade Thirteen; a holy card picturing St. Anthony with a fail-safe prayer on the back, given to her by Sister St. Anthony; all the just not quite right clothes Mumma has painstakingly made for her because store-bought were out of reach; two pairs of high-heels purchased by Cousin Bridget; a small wooden jewelry box containing the Dunkeld broach, her fake pearls, and her school ring; a photograph album with pictures dating back to Daddy in World War Two; and folded in a mauve silk scarf the only photograph she has of Teddy. He is smiling wickedly and his blue hat sits at a rakish angle on top of his clipped red curls.

Tears well. Anna has been throwing up into the toilet as quietly as she could every morning. She has missed two periods. She clasps a tattered copy of Hamlet to her chest and sobs.

She finds Mumma sitting on Mrs. Dumice's stoop. She is smoking. When she sees Anna's face her hands go out automatically. "What is it, Child?"

"I'm pregnant, Mumma."

Suddenly white, Mumma's face registers shock, then anger, an expression which Anna has never before seen on her mother's face. Then the pity flows in and the love. She gathers Anna into her thin arms. "My poor, poor child."

"I can't go to university, Mumma."

Mumma hugs her hard.

"I'll have to get married, Mumma. And I'm only seventeen."

Mumma holds her at arm's length. Her face is stern when she says, "Do you love the boy?"

"Yes."

"Can he take care of you?"

"Yes."

"Do you want to marry him? Will he marry you?"

"Oh yes."

"Then you must be very strong and accept responsibility for what you have done."

Anna's Inner Voice asks, *Did you think Mumma would have some magic to save you?*

"Yes, Mumma."

Anna returns to the house where Mumma leaves her in privacy. She picks up the telephone receiver. Teddy has given her a number to call if she has to. It is the men's mess hall at Trenton Base. A gruff male voice answers. When she asks for Airman Teddy Fisher, the voice says crankily, "Airman Fisher is not in the Mess at present, Miss."

"But it's his sister, Anna. It's a family emergency. I have to talk to him. Please. It's very important."

A little kinder now, "Well, Miss, I'll send one of the lads to find him. Give me your number and he will call back. It might be some time, though."

She gives him the number. She sits on the dusty brown chair in the living room, the black telephone on a table beside her. Her father looks down at her from his photo on the piano. She sits there for forty-five minutes. Mumma comes in with a cup of tea and leaves right away. Anna can see that Mumma's eyes are red. Pain shoots across her breasts under her pink seersucker blouse. The telephone rings.

"Anna. What is it?"

"Ogod, Teddy. I'm pregnant."

Silence. An unsteady voice, unlike Teddy's. It's all right, kid. I'll get leave. I'll beg if I have to. I'm coming. Don't worry about anything. I'm coming."

One day passes. Two. No word.

Anna is sitting on a rock out by the creek with her feet in the water when Mumma comes up behind her. She kneels beside her. It's Wednesday and Mumma is holding the local newspaper, The Dunkeld Messenger, a five-paged missive that comes out once a week. Wordlessly she hands the paper to Anna. There is a big black and grey picture on the front page. A car is wrapped around a tree. Police and ambulance men stand looking helplessly at the car. Anna can tell that the photo was taken at night by the glare of the police car lights that give the scene and eerie unreality.

The headline reads, "LOCAL YOUTH KILLED IN SINGLE CAR ACCIDENT ON HIGHWAY 41. ALCOHOL BELIEVED TO BE A FACTOR.

"A well-liked local youth was killed Monday night on the Eganville Road when his car left the highway and slammed into a tree. It is not yet known if alcohol was a factor in the accident. Friends of Teddy Fisher mourn his passing. Fisher was in the Canadian Airforce stationed at …"

Anna's world goes white and then black.

What does one do when everything one hoped for, all the dreams, all the fantasies, all the longed for love, all the girlish desires, even the difficult resolutions are ripped from one's heart without anaesthetic? What good Mumma's and Cousin Bridget's loving faces? What good Sister St. Anthony's quiet telephone call? What good Colleen's scandalized but generous tears? What good prayer? What good sitting around waiting for the world to explode into innuendo, gossip, fatuous pity, satisfied looks?

Anna puts on her rose dress, her crinolines, her white high-heeled shoes. She hitches a ride with one of the smart-aleck boys on a Saturday night. She arrives at Sunnydale Acres, searches out Kenneth Beck, dances the night away in his bony arms, and seduces him in the back seat of his pharmacist father's car. One month later she is married in the Presbyterian Church. Seven and one-half months later, Rachel Beck is born. She has her real father's red hair and his hazel eyes. The marriage lasts two years before Anna asks for and is given a divorce by a bewildered Kenneth Beck. She has Rachel baptized in the Catholic Church. Kenneth who truly loves his little daughter exchanges all argument for the peaceful right to see Rachel whenever he likes, to have her at his apartment over the pharmacy for overnight visits, to inspire her receptive little brain with the seriousness of his own. He intends, despite Anna's protest, to see that his daughter has the best education his money can buy. If it must be Catholic, so be it.

Kenneth is forever smitten by little Rachel and if it were known, Anna has unwittingly brought into his life its one true happiness.

Anna vows she will never, never, no matter what, reveal to Kenneth or Rachel who her daughter's father really is. Mumma knows. She never asked but she knows.

Anna accepts no divorce settlement for herself. To her chagrin, Teddy had left a will with a small amount of money in her name. She used it to put a stone on his grave in the Anglican cemetery. On it she had engraved, Beloved Friend, Teddy Fisher. Sometimes, she places a red rose there.

She goes to work as Assistant Librarian to Miss McKrachen who says, "You can learn anything from books, girl."

Chapter 19

COMING HOME

1965

"Made you look you dirty crook. Stole your Momma's pocketbook.""

"You are a big turd, Jimmy." Tootsie's voice drifts in through the open French doors of the library to disturb the leaden August quiet. The old-house-cool settles once again.

Anna looks across at Colleen flopped in the leather chair on the other side of the fireplace. "Even the heat doesn't slow them down, does it?"

"Fiddly fart the barber, Anna Dunkeld, they are just children."

Laughter darts up Anna's throat and she purses her lips to catch it. "Mumma used to always say that when she was annoyed."

Colleen bridles. "Say what?"

"Ffffiddly … far…" laughter wins and sprays.

Colleen tries to frown but a smile crinkles her mouth. "They really are a handful, aren't they? And I ask far too much of you, Anna."

"Don't say that, Colleen. Don't apologize for Christ's sake."

"It was not for Christ's sake, Anna."

Anna jumps up. "Stop it. Stop it. Why can't you just relax? Does everything have to be a moral battle? You can't really think that way. You who have been through so much. How can you still believe all that … stuff?"

Such an attack would usually have Colleen dissolving into tears and dire foreboding about Anna's eventual fall into perdition. But not today.

"Sit down, Anna." Colleen's voice is calm, stern. Anna sits.

Colleen puts down her knitting and leans forward, her pale, coppery hair glinting; perspiration glistening on her upper lip. "Anna why is it that only your beliefs are valid, only your feelings can make sense out of the world we live in? And you're not even consistent. One day you are praying to St. Anthony to help Mumma and the next day you are condemning me for going to Perpetual Help Devotions. You can't have it both ways."

Anna opens her mouth.

"No. Let me finish. I truly believe in my faith. I believe that if I keep trying and obey the teachings of the Church that I shall some day be rewarded. And I believe in prayer and fasting in Lent and saying novenas and … well all the rest. It gives me comfort. It keeps me going. And it is … beautiful."

"May I say something?"

"Of course."

"I do know what you mean, Colleen. It's just that I cannot condemn the things the Church condemns. And I cannot abide its attitude towards women. I don't condemn *you*, really I don't."

"I know."

"It's just that you have suffered so much. And you forgive and forgive. How could you let your husband abuse you for so long? Why didn't you shoot the bastard?"

Colleen smiles. "I thought about it."

"Weren't you scared?"

"No. I suppose I should have been but I wasn't. I'm still not. I thought I could save him, in the end. It was only when he threatened the children that I came to you and Mumma. And I loved him. You know, Anna, it's true, it's really true that there is a kernel of good in everybody unless they are completely insane or born without conscience."

"Hitler should have had a year with Sister St. Ambrose," Anna says.

Colleen laughs and Anna relaxes, feeling brave enough to ask, "Do you think you will ever love another man?"

"Who knows? There is one man. But he is taken and the woman he loves doesn't even realize he loves her."

"Colleen Dunked, you little devil. Who is it? Tell?"

"I'm just talking nonsense. Tootsie and Jimmy are enough for me."

The bell over the fireplace rings Anna and Colleen jump to their feet. They are both across the rug and out the door before the ringing stops.

They reach Mumma's room side by side. Bridget is sitting by the bed holding Mumma's wrist. Faith's small body convulses as if fighting off a thousand devils. Her eyes have rolled back, her false teeth fallen.

"Anna, call Tess. Colleen, take out your mother's teeth and hold her hand. Talk to her. She can hear you. Talk to her."

Faith survives the heart attack, her fourth.

"What is keeping her alive, Tess?" Anna asks. "I can't bear to see her suffer like that."

"Anna dear. Your mother should have died during the first attack. Her heart is finished. But she isn't? She will not die. She is not ready. Respect that. Help her in her fight. She's not afraid of the pain. You must have the same courage for her."

"I know. I know."

They are in the kitchen, everyone's favourite room. Bridget and Colleen are with Mumma. Rachel, summoned from school, has shut herself in her bedroom. Charlotte has taken the twins for a visit with her boys.

"Anna I'm worried about you."

"Me?"

"Yes, *you*. You need some pleasure, some joy in your life. You are only twenty-eight years old."

"You can say that, Tess, with my mother lying up there?"

"Bullshit."

"I don't want to talk about it. Anyway will we keep her home again?"

"Yes. There's no use moving her to hospital. It's so far away. We'll have round the clock nursing care here and I'll call in every day."

They chat for another while and Tess leaves quietly. Anna has her cry and then goes to the kitchen window. An early evening breeze wafts up from the bay and wipes her brow. Dusk has fallen under the tunnel of trees which lead to the house from the gate. Anna can see movement at the gate. Someone has opened it and stepped inside. The figure stands still for a moment as if examining the house or gathering courage, it moves slowly forward. It is small. Seems to be carrying some sort of pack. Anna squints. Leans forward. Her hand goes to her mouth. She leans until her nose touches the screen. She rubs perspiration from her eyes.

She whirls. Darts to the kitchen door. Down the steps. She is running like she hasn't run in years. She is yelling. Yelling like a mad thing.

"Emma. Emma. EMMA!"

She almost knocks Emma over with her first hug. Emma pushes her away. She looks scared, lost. "You see I was in Vancouver. I saw the Beatles. They were only on for half an hour and I sold my guitar to get the ticket and it was way up in the bleachers and there was so much screaming that I couldn't hear a thing and I couldn't find my friends and they wanted to do hard drugs and I didn't want to and there was nobody from home and it rained all the time and I heard Auntie Faith call me and I had no money and I hitchhiked and I had some trouble and I had to walk on the prairies and this family picked me up and brought me to Thunder Bay and some hippies fed me and lent me bus fare and I and I …"

"It doesn't matter, my darling girl. Nothing matters. You're home. Auntie Faith has been waiting for you. Come. I'll give you a cup of tea and a wash and we'll go to her."

"I want to go now. She won't care if I'm dirty."

"No. She won't care at all."

Faith dies that night, peacefully. Anna is with her, and Emma. Faith opens her eyes, stares at the foot of the bed, smiles, and dies.

Anna wheels the book cart into the *D* isle of the bookshelves. The village library hasn't changed a great deal since she was a child except to expand in order to hold more books. The television generation seems to have rediscovered reading. The Tolkien fantasy is always on the reserved list.

The headache strikes as they all do, suddenly and viciously. Ignore it. Ignore it. You know it's not a brain tumour or migraine. Tess has given you every bloody test in the book. *What is in my head trying to force its way out?* By the time she has finished shelving the books nausea has struck. She races for the bathroom and wretches into the toilet, but nothing comes up. She gives up and takes some codeine. Now she will be dozy and stupid all evening.

A knock at the door.

"Anna, are you all right?"

"Yes, Miss McKrachen. It's just one of my headaches."

"Open the door, Child." No use telling Miss McKrachen that one is no longer a child. Anna complies.

"Come with me. I'm going to make you a cup of tea." Since the library has just closed, Anna has no excuse to refuse and besides she doesn't really want to. Miss McKrachen will mother her in her spinsterish way and tea always helps.

They go into the inner sanctum, which contains two rocking chairs with multi-coloured shawls thrown over them, a hot plate on a rickety table under the window, which looks out onto a hedge and a birdfeeder on a pole. Two doves are pecking away at the millet in the feeder and a Blue Jay screeches his disapproval from a nearby cedar. Miss McKrachen makes the tea carefully, scalding the pot and dumping the contents into a tiny sink, dropping two teabags into the pot and pouring on boiling water. She waits silently for some time, stirs the tea and removes the teabags. No tea leaf snobbery for Miss McKrachen. No sugar, no milk. Tea is tea and to be respected as such.

When they are both sipping from delicate china mugs decorated with pink roses and blue morning glories respectively, Miss McKrachen says, "I am going to do something I seldom do, Anna Dunkeld. I am going to interfere in someone's life. I want you to answer my questions as honestly as you can and then see what you can see."

Anna nods. The headache is receding and the codeine has relaxed her.

"Firstly. Have you seen Theresa Sauvé about these headaches?"

Anna sighs. "Yes. There is no apparent physical cause for them."

"Good. Now. Have you grieved your dear Mother's death or are you trying to be strong?"

"Really, Miss …"

"Do not interrupt me, Child."

Anna sips her tea. "I guess I try to be strong but isn't that what one should do?"

"Comment si diddly spit."

Anna struggles not to laugh. Miss McKrachen's expletives are just as colourful as Mumma's used to be."

"What are you doing with your life besides living everyone else's for them?"

Anna puts down her mug. "That's not fair."

"Yes it is. Abundantly fair actually. And furthermore how long is it since you were made love to."

Anna cannot believe her ears.

"Your mouth is hanging open, Child. Some people need sex and you are one of them. See that you get some if it can be done discreetly and without hurting anyone.

"Is Rachel healthy?"

"Yes." By now Anna is too flummoxed to do anything but answer.

"She is a difficult child. Don't interrupt. She's unhappy and blames you for it. No? Let her go her own way. She is smart. Some day she will realize what you sacrificed for her but not yet. Let her grow."

Miss McKrachen rises and pours both of them more of the still fragrant tea.

She crosses to a small battered writing desk in the corner and removes a black, leather jacketed book. She comes over to Anna and places it in her lap.

"This is a journal, not written in as yet. You will write in it every day and keep it locked up so you will be free to say anything you want. You are a writer, Anna Dunkeld. I saw that when you were no bigger than a toadstool. Write. Write anything. Even if it is only a long list of complaints. Write every day. And try to say something intelligent every once in a while. Try for insight. You are too young to have many but try anyway.

"And most of all, Anna Dunkeld, I want you to remember that though you are a writer by birthright, life itself is *not a novel with you as the main character.*

"Will you do this? Not for me but for yourself?"

"Yes, Miss McKrachen." Suddenly Anna is weeping.

Miss McKrachen doesn't try to comfort her. She simply goes out and quietly closes the door.

BOOK III

Chapter 20

RACHEL

1973

"Remember the time Sister St. Ambrose sent Charlotte home because she wore an orange dress to the St. Patrick's Day concert?"

"She thought Charlotte had turned into an Orangeman, crazy old bat."

Anna and Tess are lying on blankets on the hot sand at Érable Island. The sand twinkles like seven-minute frosting that has been allowed to sit too long. They have just moved into the pines' shade. Tess can smell their pungent sap. The center of the island is deserted now since the ferry stopped running in the sixties. The farms were sold to would-be cottagers from the village, the few who could afford a big boat to bring supplies across the Ottawa. Tess has a refitted cabin cruiser in which she bums up and down the Ottawa during her month long summer vacation. Anna often wonders why she doesn't swan off to Europe like half the world but immediately decides that Tess doesn't need to see everything and everywhere in order to belong somewhere. She and her people belong here in the Valley, their home for twelve thousand years.

"You know the twins say Sister Ambrose is still lurking around the Convent, sorry, Our Lady of the Snows High." Anna wiggles until her bottom forms a comfortable hollow in the sand under the blanket. "She must be a hundred years old."

"You'd think the sight of boys in the hallowed halls and above the knees skirts on the girls would have sent her off by now." Tess laughs. "I wonder what she'd think of your home for unwed mothers."

"I do not run a home for unwed mothers. It's that darned Bitsy. She keeps bringing her waifs to me and what can I do? Anyway they look out for each other and of course you keep them healthy and Welfare pays for their room and board."

"What do Tootsie and Jimmy think?"

"Do thirteen year olds think?"

"We did, a lot."

"At least you achieved your goals."

Tess knows better than to reply to that one. "We were talking about the twins and the mothers."

Anna rolls onto her stomach. "The twins are great. They are not particularly bright but they pass their exams and they are into everything, plays, sports, trips, anything going. Colleen is proud to bursting. Everybody loves them, too. But I wonder where the hell is the angst? They never ask questions. Never did. They just absorb what they need like jolly little sponges."

"And Rachel?" Tess's tone is cautious.

"She's eighteen now. And going on ninety."

"Doesn't she go to University this year?"

"Oh yes. Kenneth is paying even though it's St. Mikes. He dotes on that girl. And do you know what they do? They read Latin together. She's teaching him."

"What do you and Rachel do together?"

"Cripes, Tess. We have nothing in common. I love her terribly but I don't even think she likes me. In fact she resents me. Why, I shall never know. There aren't even the usual reasons, Mom giving kid hell for coming in late and that sort of stuff. Rachel never breaks any rules. I wish she would. It would do us good to yell and scream at each other."

Tess takes a deep breath. "Do you resent her?"

Anna jerks upright and stares down at her friend. "What a shitty thing to say."

"It stands to reason after all. She's the reason you never got to go to university, isn't she?"

"Don't be ridiculous. My own raging hormones got me into that mess."

"And how is your love life? Still running around with that officer from Petawawa?"

"You ask the damnedest questions. Yes, I still see Bill and will until he finishes his course and goes back home to Nova Scotia. We're just pleasant conveniences to each other. I like Bill. Satisfied?"

Tess rolls over on her stomach. "Wake me in ten minutes before I burn."

At Dunkeld House, Emma is walking Beverly through the apple orchard. The trees with their hard young green apples don't offer much protection from the sun so she leads her mother out under the poplars. Cool settles over them like a benediction. Beverly bends back and points up into the whispering leaves.

"Yes. They sound pretty, don't they, Mother?"

Emma spends as much time with Beverly as she can spare from her job as a civilian secretary at the Petawawa Military Base. Gone are the days of the flower child. She has learned that military types, though somewhat naive about the outside world, can be good, fair bosses. She likes working for them and dating the best of them. There have even been a couple of offers of marriage but Emma likes her single life, and of course, there is her mother to look after.

She has the habit now of talking all the time she is with her mother. She interprets her gibberish better than anyone in the family. It is as if she and Beverly are communicating on a level shared only by the two of them. In fact, Beverly refuses to talk with most people though she seems perfectly happy probably due to the new medication Tess is trying. The violent episodes are no more. She had struck Bridget one day for trying to get her to take a pill and she particularly resented the mothers and wasn't above giving them a whack if she could reach them. Probably jealous. Now she does everything docilely. However, she talks only to Emma and asks for her incessantly, calling her *the Girl*.

Beverly leans back and points to the sky. "See them."

Emma looks up and sees nothing but a couple of clouds trespassing on the hot blue dome. "Yes. Pretty clouds."

Beverly becomes agitated. "No. No! See the … words … little things, fast … not bad …

"Do they like you?"

A smile. "Yes."

"I see them," though she sees nothing.

She notices tiny bubbles of perspiration on her mother's upper lip. "Let's sit down here on the grass where it is cool." Beverly demurs at first staring into the grass, perhaps seeing some thing lurking there. Emma sits and squirms around to flatten the grass. She stands and points to the spot. "See, nothing to hurt you."

Beverly smiles and with help sits. Emma takes her place beside her. Who is this creature beside her, certainly not the mother she has hated and feared most of her life. What twists of consciousness and disease had produced this creature … this docile creature, at least when it comes to Anna and me? Suddenly tears spurt from her eyes and she is sobbing, terrible painful sobs that rip right up from her stomach and shoot pain across her chest. *I have to stop this. I'll scare the living daylights out of her.*

But Beverly isn't scared. She bends over like a child trying to look up into Emma's face. "I'm sorry. Don't cry little girl. I didn't mean it. Don't cry."

Emma does something she hasn't done since she herself was a child. She throws her arms around her mother and sobs into her lap while Beverly smoothes her sweaty hair back from her forehead and croons, "Don't cry little girl."

When she has finally quieted Emma takes her mother's still beautiful face between her palms and says, "Listen to me, Mother. I forgive you. I forgive you. I love you."

"I love Emma." It is the first time in years that she has said her daughter's name.

Anna returns home hot and tired. Her face and shoulders feel sunburned though she knows it will not show for a few hours. She climbs the stairs to Faith's old room over the kitchen, Anna's now. She has kept it just like her mother did, with the rocking chair under the window, the old dresser with the carved leaves around the mirror brought down from the attics, the shabby bedspread with the doll-like girl and her flowers and bluebirds, loved because Faith stitched it. Anna strips, throws her clothes in the laundry basket in the cupboard over the kitchen stairs, and dons an old summer bathrobe of Faith's. It is white seersucker with tiny blue flowers, probably forget-me-nots. Many washings have made it soft and thin on the skin. She goes to the main bathroom, the old one with the claw-legged tub, the toilet on a platform, the sink from which the porcelain has been almost scrubbed away. The shower is an awkward thing on a pole, rigged by Louis. They have had two modern bathrooms installed off each end of the upper gallery but Anna prefers this relic as she prefers everything old and full of stories.

When she has showered she changes into a pair of white shorts and a sleeveless yellow top. She pads off to Rachel's room on bare feet. *Might as well get it over with.*

Rachel's door is opened and she is bending over a trunk, the same trunk Anna had once begun to pack to go to St. Mikes. Anna's breath catches and Rachel looks up.

"Oh. Hello, Mother."

"Packing?"

"It would seem so."

"Anything I can do to help?"

"No." Catching herself, probably realizing that this is bad manners. "Well, yes. Dad has given me a small framed picture of him to take with me. Perhaps you would like to give me one, too?" Seeing the surprised look on Anna's face, "I have that great group shot from when Grandmother was alive but I don't have one of you alone."

Is she reaching out to me? Is she just being polite? "Of course. I have a quite recent one in a small frame that won't take up too much room. Why did I *have to put it like that? Idiot.* Rachel's face reveals nothing. "I'm going to miss you around here. We all are. But I know you will love university. There is so much to learn. Will you study only the humanities or are you doing a science?"

"I'll have to talk with a counselor when I get there but I would like to concentrate on languages and math and perhaps the history of religions."

She is so thin and pale. Only the brilliant hair in a plait down her straight back adds colour. She is wearing a beige blouse and shorts to match. Her hazel eyes look tired. Her legs are long and lovely but pale and freckled. *Freckles just like Teddy's. Maybe I should tell her? No. No.*

"Mother are you coming to the Centennial at Our Lady's? Sister St. Anthony is coming up from Immaculata in Ottawa especially for the day. She asked Sister Marie if you would be there?"

Anna hadn't been through the old Convent since she left there as a girl. She had been to concerts, of course, and teas, both for Emma and Rachel, and their graduations, but to tour the old school, to see Sister St. Anthony.

"Yes, Rachel. I think I will attend. Will you be doing anything special?"

"I'm serving tea and carrying the banner. There's to be an old fashioned rosary procession to the grotto and special devotions in the chapel. You'll like that, won't you?"

"I shall love it. I must remind Tess and Charlotte and Bitsy to come."

A thought. "There's something I want to give you, Rachel. Just wait here. Don't go away." As if she had any intention of doing so.

Anna rushes down the hallway and up to the old attic rooms, stubbing her bare toes three times on the treads and cursing loudly. There's the old doll suitcase, covered with dust. She wipes it with a tissue from her pocket and opens it. The first thing she sees is the little fake leather pouch which contains the pearl rosary Richard had sent her from England for her first communion. Attached to it by an elastic band is a small faded envelope with childish script reading *Daddy*, in pencil. She knows it contains the letter with the lock of her hair sent for luck in bombing Germans. She lays it aside. Yes the black velvet box is there. She rubs up the velvet and lifts the lid. The Dunkeld broach winks up at her. She races down the stairs and up the hall to Rachel's room.

Out of breath, she says, "I want you to have this, Rachel," holding out the box.

Rachel walks over to her, almost reluctantly it seems. She takes the box and opens it. "This is the Dunkeld broach, isn't it, Mother? The one you gave to Emma."

Why spoil it, child? "Yes I gave it to Emma for a time, hoping it would help her through her troubles. But it rightfully belongs to you. It has been handed down through many generations. Nana Jeanne gave it to me. It has sort of a power to it." *Too much. She will think I'm crazy.*

But Rachel looks more embarrassed than anything. Awkard. Not used to such gestures from her mother. *Not used to it? What have I done?*

"Thank you, mother. I shall cherish it."

"Hell. I know you don't like to be hugged but I'm going to hug you anyway." Anna grabs her daughter and an awkward hug ensues, her own arms managing to encircle Rachel who stands stiffly but does not pull away. It is like hugging a dead sapling. When she holds her daughter at last away from her and searches her face, she sees something there. What is it? A question? A need? "Is there something wrong, Rachel?"

Rachel purses her lips. "No mother. What could be wrong? I'm going to university! I so want to go, Mother. I'm almost afraid something terrible will happen and I'll be prevented."

"Nothing will prevent it, Rachel. You will go and you will do us all proud. You'll be the first to go since your Great Grandfather Sean."

This time it is more like hugging a green willow sapling.

Anna knocks at the front door of Our Lady of Snows.

I haven't stood at this door since I was little and Mumma and I used to come to pay the monthly fee for Colleen.

An elderly nun who looks faintly familiar opens the door and welcomes her with a gracious smile. "You know the way to the chapel?" Anna nods. "The opening ceremonies will take place there."

Anna thanks her and passes into the shadowed, hushed hallway. The powerful Rembrandt-like painting of Christ on the Cross is still the first thing one sees. Enormously sad, human. She turns right and goes past Sister Margaret Mary's door and the door to the music hall, which stands open. She peeks in. The same polished floors and pianos, the same raised platform and even, she would be willing to bet, the same ferns on stands. She climbs the stairs, ghosts of little grade ones climbing beside her. She passes the statue of Our Lady of Snows which guards the classrooms. She bows before she realizes what she is doing. Up, up to the chapel. She can smell the incense. She enters, dips her fingers in the holy water font and blesses herself. There are already some women in the front pews and in the back are the nuns, heads bowed, all murmuring the rosary. Anna spies Charlotte and Tess sitting a few rows back on the side. She joins them. She kneels on the hard wooden kneelers.

Nothing has changed. The wonderful fresco of Mary surrounded by cherubs soars above the white and gold altar. To the sides are the familiar guardian angels, the statues, and *dear old friend* St. Anthony holding the Christ Child. The ruby vigil lamp hangs from the ceiling, lit. *Christ is present.* Anna joins her hands and bends her head.

O Sacrament most Holy
O Sacrament Divine
All praise and all thanksgiving
Be every moment Thine

She says a few more prayers for Mumma and her Father and Nana and Teddy and then she sits down beside Charlotte, tugging at her short skirt. She should have worn something more modest. She sees Ruby Flaherty, looking stout and prosperous, ensconced beside Colleen across the aisle.

Charlotte leans over and whispers, "You can take the girl out of the Convent but you can't take the Convent out of the girl."
Tess says, "Shut up or we'll all get the ruler."

Rachel enters holding the azure and white silk banner on a pole with ribands leading down to four Grade Twos looking pleased as posies. They are wearing blazers, blouses, and skirts but Anna sees pleated black uniforms with hard collars and cuffs and enormous black bows.

The procession weaves through memories, going very slowly so the alumnae can peek into their old classrooms, which have not changed one iota except for more modern desks in the upper grades. The kitchens, the boarders rooms, and out through the music hall to the yard and grotto. Anna feels an overwhelming sense of belonging, of peace and goodness.

How sheltered we were.

Afterwards they attend a very proper tea in the boarders' dining room. Ladies of every age and description sip from white and gold china teacups and nibble at tiny rolled sandwiches and iced petit-fours. Quite a few Valley priests hold court and the Bishop is rumoured to be coming from Pembroke to give Benediction of the Blessed Sacrament; and some village dignitaries are in attendance, even the Protestant ones. Nuns festooned in smiles greet *their girls* in clusters. Some of the nuns are wearing the new habit with short skirt and an abbreviated veil topping mostly dyed hair and old lady hairdos. Anna is shocked. She greets and hugs all of them, even the ones who seemed enemies so long ago. Sister Marie, a tiny old doll. Sister Sr. Timothy, jolly and rosy-cheeked as ever. Sister St. Stephen, still nervous and gentle. Sister St. Ambrose looking and acting like Queen Victoria. Even Sister St. Luke greeting Anna as a long-lost, beloved child.

Hasn't changed, the two-faced …

But it is Sister St. Luke who says, "Anna you must see Sister St. Anthony. She has been looking everywhere for you. I think she's up in the old Grade Thirteen classroom."

Anna is gone. Rushing up the stairs, running down the hall, puffing to a halt outside the classroom. She knocks out of old habit even though the door is open.

"Anna!" Calm and poised as ever, Sister St. Anthony floats quickly towards her. She takes both Anna's hands and tilting her head looks for a long time into her eyes. "My dear, dear girl."

She wastes no time in asking Anna about her life or her family. "Are you writing, Anna?"

"I keep a journal, Sister. And I still scribble the odd short story."

No praise or disappointment. That is not Sister St. Anthony's way. "You are well. I can see that." She gestures towards the room. "It has not changed much, has it?"

"No, Sister." *Why am I so tongue-tied? There is so much to say and I can't think of anything. Shit. Shit. Shit.*

"Walk with me down to the tea." And they go softly along the cool, dim hallway and down the stairs side by side. At the door to the dining room, Sister St. Anthony puts her hand on Anna's arm. "I must mingle with the others now. Be happy." And she is gone.

Anna wants to run after her, pull her aside, tell her all her troubles, confess her many sins. Instead she turns away wet-eyed and is overwhelmed by a flock of former school chums, hugs and smiles and squeals and perfume. *It feels so damned good. So safe.*

Then she spots him. She extricates herself and rushes over. "Charlie, you old holy roller, what are you doing here?" Charlie has moved his practice to Pembroke, the only valley town where the population has at least remained static.

"Anna!" He holds her shoulders and kisses her on the cheek. "I guess I rate as one of the Valley toffs. What a wonderful old school. No wonder you loved it so much. I even met your Sister St. Anthony. There's a real lady."

A beautiful, skinny brunette who has been standing back to back with Charlie and chatting with some older women, turns and takes his arm possessively. "So this is Anna. I have heard so much about you."

God. This must be the girlfriend. But Charlie, a snot? I know she's a snot. She reeks of money and that hairdo is too bloody perfect. She says, "You must be a friend of Charlie's."

Charlie introduces her, an old-money Ottawa name, a she-lawyer for godsakes. "Glad to meet you," Anna lies.

"I am so impressed with your little school. So historical."

Bitch. "I'm glad you like it. But I must run. So many old friends to greet. I'm pleased you came, Charlie. Don't be a stranger. Come out to the house next time you come home. Cousin Bridget and Colleen would so love to see you. And Emma." They exchange looks. Charlie had attended Mumma's funeral and seen Emma again but had never mentioned his search for her. In fact, Charlie spent more time at the Pembroke Court House and in Ottawa than he did visiting his mother in Dunkeld Village.

As if reading her thoughts, he says, "I'm spending a month or so in Ottawa on business but I'll drop by when I come back." But somehow Anna knows he won't.

Later Charlotte, Tess , Anna, and Bitsy, who arrived late but managed to make it for tea, meet as if by assignation under the old oak tree in the school-yard.

"I wish we could be kids again," Charlotte says.

Tess puts an arm around her waist. "Wouldn't it be wonderful?"

Anna says, "Join hands." Their small circle goes round and round with Bitsy in the centre.

> *Ring around the rosy*
> *A pocket gull of posies*
> *Husha, husha*
> *We all fall down*

And down on their knees they go in the dust laughing and giggling. "Sweet god. Get up. Here comes Sister St. Ambrose!"

Chapter 21

TESS

1975

They find out about Tess and they run her out of town.

Some lard-assed old biddy from the Lady's League sees Tess at a formal fund-raising dinner for the Sick Children's Hospital in Ottawa. She is accompanied by a notorious and very beautiful lesbian actress from Toronto. A few whispered conferences between the biddy and her like among the crowd and the biddy whips home to Dunkeld Village to announce that they have a pervert in their midst. Forgotten are Tess's years of dedication, the children brought squalling into the world, the soothing presence at deathbeds, the tonsils and appendix and gall bladders safely removed, the quiet talks with worried mothers, with terrified, abused wives, with troubled teens, with women fearing they are pregnant and men fearing they are impotent; forgotten is the goodness that is Tess.

She is *One of Those! What could you expect from a squaw, anyway?*

The priest speaks to the Catholic Women's League, telling them unconvincingly to be good Catholics.

The Presbyterian and Anglican ministers remonstrate quietly with the Ladies' sewing circles.

Good men speak to Tess on the street and would tip their hats if they had any. Good women invite her to tea and bridge parties to find that half their guests develop headaches and forgotten engagements.

A redneck in a turned-around cap says on the street, loud enough to be heard by Anna, "There goes that cunt whose friends with the dyke doctor.

Probably the two of them have been at it for years." Tess strides up to him stamps as hard as she can on his instep and backhands him across the face. She expects to at least find a burning cross on her lawn but soon realizes that the red neck and his other brain dead friends probably think she was mad at being called a lesbian and admire her for it.

Tess goes through it all with her usual calm dignity. She recruits a young, clever, white, straight male not long out of medical school and sells her practice to him.

"You're going where?" Anna yelps.

"Toronto. It's either that or Vancouver. As a matter of fact, I've found quite a good practice to buy into."

"Are you in love with that actress?"

"No. Actually I have been seeing a really special woman for years. She's a harpist. She is moving to Toronto with me and we can be together there without stirring up the Canadian equivalent of the KKK."

Anna realizes for the first time that Tess's moving away will leave a chasm in her life which will never be filled. "But what about me!" she yells.

"Stop shouting, Anna. I shall miss you dreadfully, you know that. But I have to live, and live with a modicum of respect and personal happiness. I could never do that in Dunkeld Village now. Anyway, you'll come to visit. You and Rachel and I can do the town together and buy outrageously expensive outfits at Holt Renfrew."

The Inner Voice prompts, *"She's right. Let her go. Let her go graciously and lovingly."* "But I don't *want* her to go."

"You could stay here. This will die down. Look at Miss McKrachen. Nobody gives her grief. And the two old ladies who live in the yellow house on River Street."

"Anna. They belong to a generation when there were many women who were forced by circumstance to take care of aged parents or who were just too homely to catch a man. People think of them as old maids and that could be what they are. If they are lesbian, chances are they don't even realize it. And if they do, they have sublimated their feelings into good works or care of others. I'm not like that. I want a relationship, which is as whole and as beautiful as anything is between men and women. I can't find that here."

"Will you come to the next reunion at the convent?"

Tess smiles and hugs Anna. "Comment si diddly spit! Of course I shall."

Anna isn't sleeping. She wakes up at 3 a.m. and goes to pee, her feet guided by the baseboard night-lights she keeps always burning in her bedroom, the hallway, and the bathroom. Of course she is not afraid of the dark. That is for children. But she just feels more comfortable when alone if blank blackness does not envelop her world. Sometimes she sits in Mumma's rocking chair by her open window and peers into the night, the cool, whispering dark caressing her face and breasts. Sometimes this works and she falls asleep again when she returns to her bed and performs the ritual of straightening sheets, plumping her pillow just so, curling like a snail with her right hand under the pillow and her eyes closed. She tells herself a story. It doesn't even matter what the story is about except that it is best to make it a serial story, which can be continued before sleep every night.

Some nights this works.

Other nights she finally leaps angrily from the bed and finds the latest sleep book, not too interesting lest it engage her brain too much, props her pillows and reads until her head has dropped to her chest at least three times. Then she turns out the light, curls up like a snail, puts her right hand under her pillow, and tries once more to sleep.

But there are the nights when her brain leaps about like a field mouse on snow. She remembers Mumma and the long years of suffering. *Why didn't I stop her smoking? Richard. Why did he have to always help everyone whether they deserved it or not? If he hadn't tried to cross the ice to Érable Island that night …* I did a bad job with Emma, too. Anything might have happened to her. And Rachel? How can I reach her? Should I tell her about Teddy? *I don't know!* And Tess. Those bastards. She's so good. She's everything I ever wanted to be.

What I need is a man. *And just what good would that do? Remember how you felt the last time an affair was over. So much time wasted.* Why can't I be like Mumma was? Why didn't I stop her smoking …?

When she finally gets to sleep she has nightmares in which the old house on Maple Street is sinking into a quagmire of mud and Richard won't listen when she tries to tell him and Mumma looks at her with indifferent eyes.

The days are better. She is able to be quite pleasant with the mothers, of which there are two at the moment, one sullen and one bouncy and cheery. The new doctor takes care of them and will deliver their babies just as Tess had. Anna avoids Cousin Bridget who will tell her that she is getting skinny. Bridget is in her sixties now and looks much older because her great weight and her arthritis make her move about ponderously on two canes. The stairs are impossible for her so Anna has moved the mothers to the old nursery and Bridget and Louis to a corner of the main floor ballroom, which has remained unfurnished and closed off for many years. Louis built a privacy partition around the ballroom fireplace and a smaller room with raised toilet and a shower with plenty of invalid handles. They got some Wanders (a name Anna applies to all lost young men) to move Bridget's heavy furniture and her many pictures and ornaments into the partitioned room which actually is quite cozy and sunlit by the two tall ballroom windows it encloses. Heating might become a problem in winter even with the fireplace but they'll face that problem when it arises. Louis insists on sleeping on a simple cot outside Bridget's door in case she needs him during the night or she is well enough for them to make the deeply passionate, slow and precious love which is life's reward for older couples.

Colleen moves like a shadow through the house, always just leaving a room as Anna enters. She is content now in her solitary life. The old nervousness seems gone and a new serenity has taken its place. The twins come home only to meals, if then. Anna loves to hear their noisy entrances. Beverly died quietly in her sleep just after the previous Christmas. Everyone was glad that her last years had been peaceful and without fear. Jimmy has taken over her old room looking out over the bay and Tootsie has Anna's old room. After her mother's death, Emma, beautiful in her new maturity, had left her job in Petawawa and moved to Ottawa where she works for the government. She writes that she has met a nice man, a social worker who seems really to care for his charges. His name is Sam. She says he reminds her of Uncle Charlie.

Rachel is home from university for the summer but her room is empty. She has taken a job at the Petawawa Military Base in the PX coffee shop and rented a room in Petawawa Village. She makes duty visits to Anna, riding up on the Colonial Coach Line bus after telephoning Anna to meet her in front of the Dunkeld Hotel. This always happens on a Sunday. Anna gives her late lunch in the kitchen and they talk about school and the job. When Anna asks her about the future, Rachel always says she doesn't know yet. At three o'clock Anna drives her to see Kenneth in Pembroke. He will later take her to the evening bus. Rachel always fits in a visit to Bridget who spends most of her days in her room, wanders out to find Louis working in the garden, and visits with the twins if they are home. Colleen usually makes some excuse about lunch so that Anna and Rachel can be alone together. It's often a need to take care of the flowers at the church.

Rachel is growing into a beauty. She is tall, slender, and willowy. Her titian hair still falls in a braid down her back but that back is less stiff now. She still wears classic style clothes and on her slim body the simple lines flow attractively.

"You are looking rather gaunt, Mother. You're not ill, are you?"

"No, Dear. I'm fine." Anna plays with the shrimp salad she has prepared especially for Rachel who loves seafood.

"How is everything at the library?"

"The same as ever. Miss McKrachen never changes." In fact, Miss McKrachen leaves Anna quite alone and Anna suspects her of waiting for something. "And you wouldn't believe how busy we are. I swear Dunkeld Village is becoming book hungry."

"Do you see much of Tess in Toronto?"

"She takes me and my roommate out to dinner about once a month. Aunt Tess knows all the best places to eat. And she bought me this dress." It is a traditional shirtwaist with a narrow skirt, the dusty blue colour flattering to Rachel.

"Tess always had good taste."

Rachel takes a bite of salad and stares at the tablecloth during the ensuing silence. She looks ups. "Mother, are you sure you're all right?"

"My dear child. Of course I'm all right. I've just had trouble sleeping lately and it makes me look dragged out but I'm as healthy as a pig."

"Maybe you should take something to sleep."

"I will if I ever become desperate but I'm sure it's just a temporary aberration."

Anna is wondering when the roles of mother and daughter became reversed.

"Anyway, finish your salad. I want to show you the meadows. The wildflowers are phenomenal this year. Remember how you and the twins used to play out there?"

They meander hip deep among the wildflowers, a cool breeze wafting from the woods beyond the meadows. It looks like someone else has been walking there for there are paths among the daisies, black-eyed Susans, wild aster, milkweed, cornflower, Canterbury bells, and St. Ann's lace. Anna will have to tell Louis to watch out for trespassers. Old Man Logan is long dead but one never knows. Mother and daughter are silent, their mutual love of nature a quiet bond.

The depression gets worse. Anna finds herself weeping for no reason, periods of blank calmness alternating with irrational anger, which she must swallow. Is she going to become another Miss McKrachen? And would that be so terrible? She hears Sister St. Anthony's voice. *Write.* And what good would that do? Who would want to read anything she wrote? Her journal is becoming a cesspool of self-pity and gloom. If only she had a kindred soul with whom to talk. But Tess is gone. She thinks of Charlie. Sure. Since his mother died, Charlie never comes to Dunkeld Village. Instead he gallivants about in Ottawa most of the time with a different bimbo on his arm every month … that is if one can believe the Dunkeld biddies. There are no interesting men in the village and Anna is tired of meaningless flings with army officers.

Oh Mumma, if only you were here.

Chapter 22

THE WRITER

1976

A library book sets Anna off on her first novel. She has been writing religiously in her journal for years, keeping it locked in a box hidden in the dresser with the oval mirror. Tucked among its pages is the picture of Teddy in his blue hat. Six months after she began to confide her secrets to the journal, her terrible headaches lessened and now they are a thing of the past.

"If anyone ever finds my journal though, I'm up the creek."

Though her depression has lifted, the many short stories she has written have been unanimously rejected by all the good literary magazines though a couple have been printed in obscure, short-lived rags. The local paper will take anything she offers whether it be an historical vignette or a description of a town meeting or even a bad poem. However, Anna does not want to write non-fiction.

She takes the fatal library book down from the shelf for a school child needing information on dinosaurs and decides it is too advanced for the child. Bored by a slow day at the library she leafs through the book. It is in reality an anthropological study of ancient man and animals, a finely illustrated, charted, and researched book at university level. What a story! This is beyond her experience. She is immediately immersed in human evolution, physical anthropology, Neanderthals, the Stone Age, the Ice Ages, Paleolithic art, Pleistocene Glacial Ecology, the origins of language, native legends, the flora and fauna of the Ice age on the Canadian Shield when the first North Americans were travelling the ice corridor from Beringia to southern Canada … and on … and on …

Requests for books go out to all the Valley libraries and then to the Ottawa ones. But it is a book by a Valley anthropologist that casts Anna into a world of ancient volcanoes that gradually formed the oldest mountains on earth, her own beloved Laurentians; tells the tale of an ancient sea that covered the Valley and the birth at its recession of the majestic Ottawa River; but best of all reveals the mesmerizing tale of how the first ancient men and women ventured into the Valley and remained there until discovered by French explorers. They were her own beloved Algonkin, *Tess's and Louis's people!*

She will write about them. She will begin her first novel.

The loneliness after Rachel's and Tess's departures turns into a hunger to know and to create. She rushes home every day from the library, gulps down her dinner and hurries across the hall where her manual typewriter squats on an old oak refectory table in the morning room. It is a calming room with faded rose wallpaper, off-white draperies, a number of scuffed antique chairs and settees, and an expanse of oak flooring burnished by generations of polishing. Anna has commandeered the room from the mothers, handing the games room, home of the large coloured television and the twins' nefarious activities, over to them for their chats and visitors. She wonders what the ghosts of early nineteenth century billiard players think of this round-bellied invasion.

Anna has to sit on a cushion and place her feet on a stool to get to the proper height for typing, but the morning room's side windows look out on Dunkeld Bay with its dancing blue waters, rocky edge, and pretty white birches on the far shore. The perfect place to write. Serene and sunny. For further inspiration she has set on the windowsill the old papier-mâché elephant given to her by Nana Jeanne. The elephant, the daisy, and the ladybug have become her charms outclassed only by St. Anthony himself.

At last Anna is officially lost in the land of stories, her very own stories. Her Inner Voice stops carping about her everyday failings and whispers to her of ancient times and things of purity and wonder. She intends to make Tess the heroine of her novel but another woman, real and unpredictable and brave and cowardly and scared and happy and loved and hated is born, and she and her companions take over Anna's mind and her inner life.

I wonder what Mumma would think? And Nana Jeanne? Richard would be proud.

Rachel graduates with honours from the University of Toronto. Anna and Colleen attend and Tess comes with a quiet little thing with big round glasses and long beautiful fingers. This must be the harpist. Rachel proudly conducts them around twenty-nine Queen's Park, a wonderful old Victorian mansion that has been her home for three years. The St. Joseph nuns who run this girls' residence for St. Mikes are open and friendly. They have good things to say about Rachel.

"I want to go to teacher's college if that's all right," Rachel says to Anna after the long ceremony in Convocation Hall and the obligatory photographs of room-mates and friends on the lawns. Anna has noticed that with these people Rachel is a different person. Quieter than the other squealing girls but obviously liked and sought out. Quite a few young men come up, too, to be introduced to Anna. Rachel is friendly with all but there are no obvious vibes with any one boy.

She hasn't fallen in love yet, Anna decides.

She says, "Of course, teachers' college is a wonderful idea. What will you teach?"

"Languages and History."

Just as I would have. "Your grandfather would be so proud of you today, Rachel. I wish you had known him."

"Grandmother Faith always said you were like him, Mother."

"I? If only one little bit of me were like him, I would be very glad."

Tess comes over to envelop Rachel, bouquet of roses and all, in a big embrace. "We are so proud of you!" The harpist adds her shy congratulations and Colleen puts her arm across the girl's shoulder, the two bright heads catching sun-rays. Tess puts her hand on Rachel's other shoulder and grabs Anna. "If you ladies have no plans for this evening I shall take all of us out to dinner at the Park Plaza."

At dinner Anna notices an oval-shaped, silver locket hanging between Rachel's breasts. Seeing her glance, Rachel says, "Uncle Charlie sent it. Isn't it wonderful? It was his mother's. He says she would have liked me. She's dead you know."

"I know. She was a silent, special lady, straight-backed and beautiful, a little like your mother, Tess." Tess's mother has been dead for many years. The two friends are quiet for a moment.

The harpist, sensing that this nostalgia may hide some sadness, says brightly, "And where do you intend to teach when you leave Teacher's College, Rachel?"

"If they will have me, I would like to teach at Immaculata in Ottawa."

Anna holds her face still but disappointment churns in her stomach. She had hoped that Rachel would teach in Dunkeld or even at Our Lady's High in Pembroke to be near Kenneth. She says nothing.

Home in Dunkeld Anna spends a lot of time wandering under the trees and in the meadow. Rachel has opted for the two year summer course rather than a year at Ontario Teacher's College so she will be home only for a short time before leaving for Immaculata in September.

Anna comes across Louis in the meadows, picking stones for a rock garden.

"Fine day," she says not expecting an answer from the taciturn Métis.

He nods his greying head.

"You love this place, don't you, Louis?" she blurts.

He waits so long to answer that she expects he won't, but he says finally, "It's a home to me."

"Do you ever miss the reservation and Algonquin Park?" Anna is secretly grilling him for material for her book.

"Sometimes."

A long silence.

"I'm sorry, Louis. I didn't mean to pry." Which is exactly what she has been doing.

A little smile.

"Have you noticed that someone walks periodically in the meadows?"

"Might have."

"Do you know who it is?"

Such a long silence that Anna begins to turn away. "Just some lad from the village. Don't mean any harm."

This is high praise coming from Louis.

"I just wondered."

"Louis would you do me a favour? Would you take me to pick wild blueberries on the Petawawa plains next summer? I'd rather do that than go to the berry farms."

"Might if I'm still around."

Anna goes off feeling happier. There are times that she thinks Louis actually might approve of her.

Anna is writing like mad in the drawing room when she hears distant Church bells in the village. All three churches are bonging away and it's a Monday. A fire? She runs to the window to look for smoke. Distant thunder rumbles over the Laurentians and the Ottawa. Already the sky is blackening above Dunkeld House. She runs to the telephone but the exchange is so busy she can't get through. Anxiety grows. She tears into the yard calling for Louis. Wind pounces from the northwest. There is no rain yet but the storm's coat-tails are sweeping into the bay though the worst of it will follow the river.

"What is it?"Louis shakes his head. "Surely they wouldn't ring the bells for a storm."

Colleen bangs open the kitchen door. "You stay here with Cousin Bridget and the mothers, Colleen. Louis and I are going to the village. I'll call you as soon as I know anything."The twins are in the village.

Louis is already backing the Ford out of the stable. Anna scrambles in beside him. The seat is hot even though the air is turning cool from the sudden wind. Rain begins to pelt the windshield as they drive through the gate. A blinding flash and on its tail a crash. By the time they reach the village the storm is at its height, with trees bending double and here and there branches and whole tree limbs thrown about on lawns and in the street. But the main street is all but deserted. Anna sees Mr. Butters from the hotel standing in the doorway.

"Stop, Louis!"

She dives out and is wet to the skin before she reaches the hotel man. The church bells clang on.

"What is happening?"she shouts over the thunder.

Mr. Butters, one of the men who had been kind to Tess, is a roly-poly, bald fellow with creamy skin, well named. "It's that steamer those Ottawa folks run for tourists and picnics. Some say it's sunk."

Sudden terror. A group of businessmen from Pembroke had talked some moneyed folks from the Capital City into floating an old ferry on the Ottawa between Dunkeld Village and Pembroke. The spectacular river-lakes and the beaches of Érable and Alumette Islands would attract money to the Valley, they said. Charlie was one of them.

She leaps back into the car, sodden hair tendrils hanging in her eyes, her shoes squelching. "Head for the dock, Louis. Oh hurry."

It is as dark as dusk and figures dart everywhere on the dock, slabs of rain obscuring them. Louis grabs a man dashing by with an armful of orange life belts. The man blurts, "The damned ferry. Gone down with all hands. Full of tourists. Have you got a boat at the dock?"

"A punt."

"We'll take anything. Here grab some of these life-belts. There are people everywhere in the water but they won't last long in this storm." Louis abandons the car and Anna and starts to run. She pelts after the two men. Other men and teenagers scramble everywhere. Middle aged women stand in dripping groups, sheltering under umbrellas. Some are holding orange and yellow raincoats like tents over their neighbours. Boats of every shape and condition are putting off from the dock. Some are already returning, huddled forms in lifejackets crowded aboard. Many hands reach to pull the survivors ashore and then the boats shear off to search for more. Lightening stabs at the boats but miraculously misses.

Anna grabs a man she recognizes, a lawyer from Pembroke. "Was Charlie Stuart on the ferry?" she shouts over the wind and thunder.

His head tilts. Rain rivulets run down his face. "Yes, Anna."

"Is he all right?"

"I don't know, child. There weren't enough lifejackets. He made me take this."

The storm passes and twenty-seven grateful people are pulled from the Ottawa. Charlie Stuart is not among them.

Anna will not let Louis drive her home. She runs down the road between the forests, choking and sobbing and screaming when she can breathe, "Damn you, God! You don't exist. And you, St. Anthony. I hate you. I shall never pray to you again! There is no God. It is all a crock of SHIT!"

When she staggers into the yard at Dunkeld House, Colleen is standing in the kitchen doorway. O damnation. I forgot to phone Colleen. "I'm so sorry," she wails, falling into her sister's arms.

"It's all right Anna. The twins are here. Everyone is safe."

Not everyone.

Anna pushes past Colleen and stumbles up the kitchen stairs to collapse on Mumma's bluebird bedspread.

Some hours later she awakes to find Louis bending over her. "Wake up, girl. He's all right. They pulled him out of the river at Bird Rock. He was hanging on to a big old wooden bench, the only thing that floated on that goddamned ferry."

"Charlie? He's alive. He's safe? Ohgod. Ohgod. Ohgod."

"Swallowed half the river but he'll do."

For once Louis lets a woman hug him and doesn't say a thing.

Chapter 23

OBLIGATORY LOVE SCENE

1976

The Pembroke General Hospital hasn't changed much since Anna and Tess and Charlotte helped conduct visitors through it during the grand opening in the fifties. The girl at reception is a stranger but has the look of the Beamishes from Mattawa. Anna wastes as much time as she can talking with her and then takes the stairs to the second floor. She recognizes every one of the three starched nurses at the rotunda desk, former Convent girls all. There are no nun-nurses about. Anna is glad of this. She doesn't feel up to nunnish civilities. One of the nurses is a younger sister of Charlotte's.

"Hi, Anna. Come to see Charlie? He's in number 14 down the hall."

Even they know.

Anna makes three attempts to go into Charlie's room until finally forced to do so by the sound of nurse's shoes squishing in her direction. He's sitting up in bed looking as healthy and contented as a pig in a wallow. Anna is about to chide him about getting half killed in storms and instead bursts into tears.

"Well, for the obligatory love scene," says Charlie, "that's a damp start. We holly rollers expect a bit of *euphoria.*"

Anna goes over to the bed. "Wha … wha …?"

"No. No, girl. This is where you say, *Oh my darling, all these years I have loved only you and didn't know it. When I thought you were lost forever in the merciless storm, pain shattered my broken heart and I realized that it had been you, and only you since we were two fat little kids smoking oak leave cigarettes under the hedge."*

"I don't love you."Hiccough. "I hate you."

"Well that's a start. The only trouble is I can't leap out of bed and ravish you with nuns lurking in the chapel. I'm lucky they let a holy roller in here in the first place."

Anna starts to laugh and throws herself on his chest, upsetting a urinal on a stool, urinal luckily empty. "I do love you, you big shit."

Charlie holds her away from him and stares sternly into her red, swollen eyes. "Now just a minute. I want some definite testimony here. You now realize what an idiot you have been for over twenty years? Don't interrupt. You have gotten over that randy Teddy Fisher, never to be forgotten of course but now a fond memory? You are not going to abscond with some short-haired idiot with medals on his chest? I no longer have to haul bimbos home to make you jealous? And I no longer have to haunt your back forty summer and winter like a love-sick moose? In short. You, Anna Dunkeld, are in love with me, Charlie Stuart."

"Yes, Charlie."

"Well, it's about time."

THE HAPPY BEGINNING

158